# The
# Official Papers

Into the matter known as –


# 'The Hound of the Baskervilles'

(DCC/1435/89 refers)

# About the Author

**Kieron Freeburn** was born in London in 1955 and went on to attend St. Ignatius Grammar School in Enfield, North London. He later followed in his father's footsteps by joining the Metropolitan Police in 1978.

An instinct for the work of the Criminal Investigation Department saw him selected for detective duty in 1981 and during a 19 year CID career he was involved in many major investigations including numerous cases of murder and other violent crimes throughout East and North London.

A transfer in 1990 to the Serious, International and Organised Crime Group at New Scotland Yard saw him investigate offences as far afield as Borneo, Malaysia, Singapore and the UAE.

Having left the police service he now lives deep in rural Devon with his family and, in complete contrast to his previous existence now lives a sedate life as a partner in a business that operates a fleet of classic Rolls Royce cars for weddings and themed luxury picnic tours.

He is a member of the Sherlock Holmes Society of London and a number of other Holmesian groups.

# The
# Official Papers

## Into the matter known as –

# 'The Hound of the Baskervilles'

**(DCC/1435/89 refers)**

By

Kieron Freeburn

Paperback ISBN 9781907685163
eBook (ePub) ISBN 9781907685170
Mobipocket/Kindle ISBN 9781907685187

Published in the UK by MX Publishing
335 Princess Park Manor, Royal Drive, London, N11 3GX
www.mx-publishing.co.uk

Cover design by www.staunch.com

# Dedication

This book is dedicated to my family.

# Contents

## Chapter One

**The Official reports –**

## Chapter Two

**The Police witness statements –**

# Chapter Three

**Other correspondence –**

# Chapter Four

**Official photographs –**

# Chapter Five

**Miscellaneous –**

# Chapter Six

**Explanatory Notes**

# Introduction

At the conclusion of a criminal investigation, a wealth of material is often brought together in compiling the definitive case report. In some instances this can result in room after room full of documents amassed over months or years, having to be indexed and cross-referenced against the body of the report in order to be read and digested by those considering the case.

In more normal circumstances a file would comprise several hundred pages and for ease of transfer or storage, important papers and case reports are kept together in outer covers manufactured from strong card, called 'dockets' which are indexed, copied and then filed centrally at the General Registry at New Scotland Yard. By convention, such papers are compiled in chronological order, the original report at the very bottom, the most recent addition available to be read first at the top of the folio.

The original files for many of the most celebrated criminal investigations are stored today in this very fashion, files from the days of Dr. Crippen, Jack the Ripper and even Lord Lucan sit in ordered rows of buff covers tied securely with ribbon referred to as treasury tape.

After 19 years in the CID in London I had seen enough of these files to know exactly what it was I had stumbled upon in an obscure Exeter auction room in early 2010. What I was not prepared for was the discovery of the original police papers into the matter recorded simply as – DCC/1435/89, known more readily to us as - 'The Matter of the Hound of the Baskervilles'.

In this book I have set out the papers for ease of reading in terms of chronology, starting with the receipt of Holmes' Telegram at New Scotland Yard requesting that Detective Inspector Lestrade assist him in Devonshire.

These original police reports chronicle the progress of the investigation from the police perspective, something never seen before. The folio consists of reports from the Metropolitan Police and the Devon County Constabulary as well as the Governor of HMP Dartmoor and the Pathologist who examined both Sir Charles Baskerville and Arthur Selden.

The folio concludes with police witness statements from all of the principals together with numerous items of private correspondence and even some original photographic plates.

The 'copperplate' style of handwriting from the time might prove a little taxing at first, but persevere and you will be treated to a unique insight into the workings of the police and a hitherto unseen side to the investigation into The Hound of the Baskervilles.

Form 705

## Devon County Constabulary

## REGISTERED COVER

DCC _1435/89_

NOTE.: This cover should be used only for registered correspondence

| Referred to | Date | Referred to | Date |
|---|---|---|---|
| Ch. Constable | 2/11/89 | | |
| | | | |
| | | | |
| | | | |
| | | | |
| | | | |
| | | | |
| | | | |
| | | | |
| | | | |

Minutes are not to be written on this cover; discussion is to be conducted by means of the authorised MINUTE SHEET

**DO NOT FOLD**

# Chapter One

# The Official Reports

Deposited at Grimpen Post Office at 12.08 pm

On Sun 5th May 1889 at 03.40hrs arrived

Baskerville Hall. Met by Dr Mortimer and

Mr J Barrymore. Escorted from the hallway into

the boot room where I was shown the lifeless body

of a man whom I knew in life to be Sir Charles

Baskerville. Abrasions to both palms and face

(contorted in a grotesque fashion) eyes and mouth

set wide open. Deceased dressed in a tweed suit, both

knees were scuffed as were the toecaps of both boots.

Flesh was cold but rigour-mortis was not present.

Barrymore searched for Sir C. found on gravel

path at 00.10hrs 100yds from house face down

believed dead. Dr Mortimer summoned by Perkins

Arr at 01.05hrs pronounced life extinct. Body

removed to boot room by Dr M and Mr B. I

examined pathway, nothing untoward, marks on

gravel where body fell, no other signs of disturbance

Left Baskerville Hall at 04.58hrs, returned to

Buckfastleigh Pol Station arriving at 05.50hrs

PS

| Mortuary | Tavistock | Date of Examination | 6th May 1889 |
|---|---|---|---|
| Deceased | Baskerville, Henry Sir | Date of Birth | 16th February 1843 |
| Place of Death | Baskerville Hall | Date of Death | 4th May 1889 |
| Examined By | Prof. J. Kennedy | Released for Burial | 7th May 1889 |

Physical Examination –

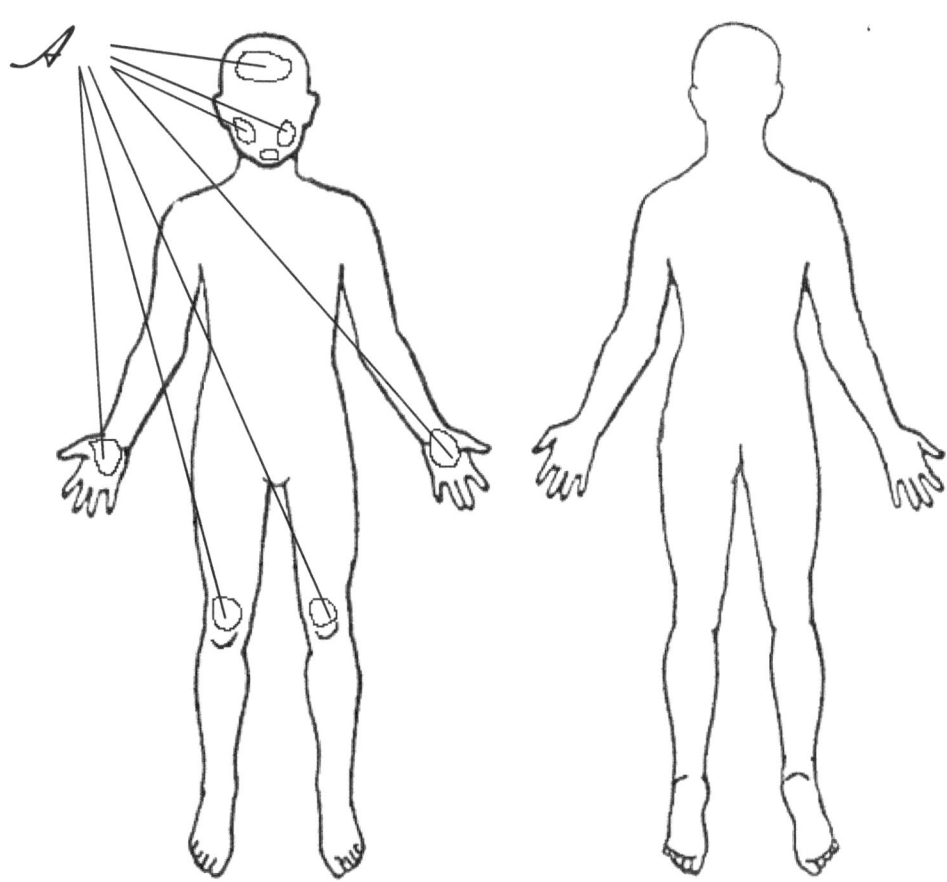

I conducted my examination at Tavistock Mortuary commencing at 09.50pm. The corpse was identified to me by Police Constable 441 Waering of Devon County Constabulary as being that of Sir Charles Baskerville.

I was assisted by a Mr Sharp, Mortuary Assistant who prepared the abdominal cavity for inspection.

Rigour mortis was still evident and on preliminary examination I noted that the facial features were wildly contorted. There were lacerations to the forehead, left and right cheeks and chin. Lesser grazes were evident on both knees. Both palms were heavily grazed and there were traces of gravel adhering to the palm tissue. These various marks are identified at A on the diagram.

On examination of the internal organs I immediately noted the heart was oversize and on dissection I found the coronary artery to be almost completely congested.

There were no other signs of illness or degeneration in any other vital organs and health was otherwise good.

Determination –

I conclude that Sir Charles Baskerville died as a consequence of myocardial infarction, the injuries to the face and hands being consistent with the deceased falling forwards onto a rough surface.

Professor James Kennedy

# Her Majesty's Prison Dartmoor

Princetown, Dartmoor, Devon

Date – *1st October 1889*

Ref –

From – *Dr. Henry Waterman, Governor*

To – *Chief Constable, Sir Charles Farrar, Devon County Constabulary*

*Sir, It pains me to report the escape of one of the inmates between the hours of 15.35 and 19.40hrs this day.*

*Arthur George Selden, Prisoner1882D (Cro 14184/89G) was convicted of Murder at the Central Criminal Court on28th August 1888.*

*He made good his escape by means unknown and is thought to be at large on the moor to the East of Princetown. My guards are conducting a search in accordance with our agreed plans; however, I would be most grateful for the assistance of the local borough constables. Might they be sent direct to the prison for a briefing.*

*H. Waterman, Governor*

# DEVON COUNTY CONSTABULARY

## SPECIAL GAZETTE

## ESCAPED CONVICT

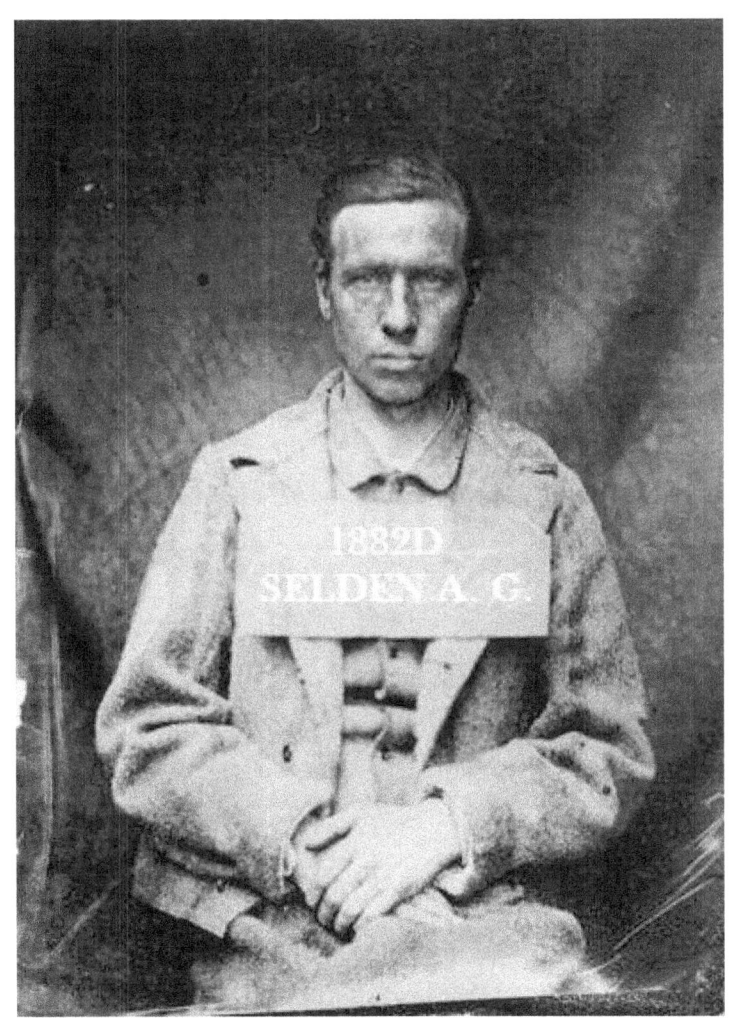

SELDEN, Arthur  5' 10"

MURDERER AT LARGE

FROM PRINCETOWN PRISON

SINCE 15th OCTOBER

REPORT ALL SIGHTINGS TO A CONSTABLE

Prefix       Code

Office of Origin and Service Instructions.

GPO Grimpen

URGENT

POST OFFICE TELEGRAPHS.

(Inland Telegrams)

| Words. | Sent. |
|---|---|
| 24 | At 08.58 M. |
| Charge. 1/- | To _____ By _____ |

NOTICE.—This Telegram will be accepted for transmission subject to the Regulations made pursuant to the 2nd Section of the Telegraph Act, 1863, and to the Notice printed at the back hereof.

12 words, 6 D. Every additional word 1½ D. Every word telegraphed is charged for whether in address or text.

TO { Detective Inspector Lestrade,CID Scotland Yard, London

| Urgent, | make | haste | GWR | to |
|---|---|---|---|---|
| Coombe | Tracey. | Will | meet | upon |
| arrival. | Danger | at | hand, | assistance |
| to | apprehend | murderer. | Bring | warrant. |
| Holmes | | | | |

FROM { Mr S. Holmes Esq. .

The Name and Address of the Sender, IF NOT TO BE TELEGRAPHED, should be written in the Space provided at the Back of the Form.

(Printed by McCORQUODALE & CO. Limited)

# Metropolitan Police

Reference ( C.O                    District / Branch **C.O**

to papers ( 

( Dist                    Station

Registry Folio No.                    *17th October* 18**89**

G.O. / Police Order                    refers

Re *Request for assistance from Mr S Holmes*

*(1)*

*Detective Chief Superintendent*

*I beg to report that a telegram has been received at Scotland Yard requesting the assistance of this officer to travel outside the Metropolitan Police District in a matter that appears to be of some urgency. The telegram was received this very morning, the sender being Mr. Sherlock Holmes of 221b Baker Street London but originating from the G.P. Office in Grimpen, Devonshire. The original document is attached to this report.*

*It asks that this officer makes urgent haste to Coombe Tracey in Devonshire to meet directly with Mr Holmes in order to assist him with a criminal investigation. It is also asked that the officer should bring an arrest warrant, unsigned, for the capital offence of Murder.*

**All minutes to be numbered in consecutive order. Continue on other side if necessary**

M.P.89 (E)

*A*

This officer respectfully seeks authority to depart London by Great Western Railway for Coombe Tracey Devonshire in order to furnish all lawful assistance to Mr Holmes.

Respectfully Submitted

G Lestrade

G. Lestrade

Detective Inspector 704

Criminal Investigation Department

Scotland Yard

(2)

Detective Chief Superintendent

I beg to report that having spoken with Detective Inspector Lestrade and having examined the telegram for myself, whilst appearing at first glance a most irregular request, it does appear that Mr Holmes is in some urgent need of the assistance of Scotland Yard. Any such warrant as mentioned would, of course, be signed by the appropriate authority in Devonshire.

Detective Inspector Lestrade has been instructed to secure himself a sidearm from the armoury and to maintain regular contact with his superiors as best he can.

All minutes to be numbered in consecutive order. Continue on other side if necessary

10

I conclude there is merit in Detective Inspector Lestrade's request.

Submitted as at 'A.

M Kellenson
Detective Chief Inspector
Criminal Investigation Department
Scotland Yard

3

I find it most irregular that one of my officers should be deployed in such a manner without the support of, let alone the knowledge of, the Devon County Constabulary.

I insist upon Lestrade making contact with the senior local detective officer at the earliest opportunity and ask that the full facts are to be reported to me without delay.

On that basis authority is granted as at 'A'.

R Steel
Detective Chief Superintendent
Criminal Investigation Department
Scotland Yard

All minutes to be numbered in consecutive order. Continue on other side if necessary

11

# Metropolitan Police

Reference     ( C.O                                    District / Branch **C.O**

to papers     (

               (   Dist     **DCC/1435/89**                      Station

Registry  Folio  No.                                   12ᵗʰ November 18**89**

G.O. / Police Order                          refers

Re     *Result of enquiries in Devonshire*

*(1)*

*Detective Chief Superintendent*

*I beg to report the outcome from my travel to Devonshire to assist Mr Sherlock Holmes in pursuance of a request as detailed in the report at 1'A' of these papers.*

*I departed London Paddington Railway Station at 10.00hrs on 18ᵗʰ October arriving without incident at Coombe Tracey Railway Station, Coombe Tracey, Devonshire at 17.05.hrs where I was met in person by Mr Sherlock Holmes and his assistant Doctor Watson.*

*From the train we adjourned to a local hostelry where I was appraised of the facts of the case by Mr Holmes. I do not propose to detail the case in this report but instead direct you to the report reference DCC/1435/89 attached at '3' to these papers, a full case report from Detective Superintendent Johns to the Chief Constable of the Devon County Constabulary dated 1st November 1889.*

M.P.88 (E)

All minutes to be numbered in consecutive order. Continue on other side if necessary

That report details the circumstance of the case in full.

In terms of the direct involvement of Scotland Yard, immediately after taking refreshment this officer together with Mr Holmes and Dr. Watson made directly on foot across moorland under cover of darkness to the close vicinity of a detached stone farmhouse known as Merripits House, owned and occupied by a Mr and Mrs Stapleton.

I had been instructed to be alert to the imminent departure from the house of one Sir Henry Baskerville who had been visiting as a dinner guest and whose own property, Baskerville Hall lay some two miles distant to the South. I was given to understand that on his departure an attack might be made upon his life.

I had travelled with a service revolver (Browning 667) drawn from the armoury together with six numbered rounds. My position was crouched in amongst boulders, my revolver drawn. Just after 10pm a thick fog began to envelop the house and with it our position and so we withdrew approximately one half-mile to higher ground.

A short time later I heard approaching footsteps and then saw the figure of a man whom I now know to be Sir Henry Baskerville passing close by along the pathway. My instructions were to hold fast and wait.

As Sir Henry set off behind our position I immediately became aware of a sound of something following in his tracks. I then saw a massive, ferocious hound race along the track in the direction that Sir Henry had taken.

All minutes to be numbered in consecutive order. Continue on other side if necessary

13

After a momentary delay Mr Holmes and Dr. Watson broke cover and made off after the beast, revolvers in hand and each fired a shot on the move. I followed at a short distance behind and saw Mr Holmes fire a further five rounds into the flank of the beast whereupon it fell. At that moment I noticed the body of Sir Henry, prone beside the hound, however, he was attended to by Dr. Watson and found to be only superficially wounded where the hound had clawed him about the collar.

I observed as Mr Holmes examined the carcass of the hound and noticed as he did so a luminescence around the mouth. I am advised that this resulted from a phosphor preparation being applied to make the teeth of the hound glow, even in darkness.

We continued to Merripits House where a search revealed in an upstairs room a female whom I now know to be Mrs Stapleton, bound to a timber beam. On being attended to by Dr. Watson there was evidence of recent injury to her person, injuries she attributed to her husband of whom there was no trace.

The immediate area consisted mainly of foul bog known as Grimpen Mire and covered an expanse of several miles. I am advised that the terrain is so treacherous that a man could be lost by stepping just feet from the pathways. The only discovery of note was a man's boot found close to the path which has subsequently been identified as belonging to Sir Henry having been mislaid, though, in London during his stay at the Northumberland Hotel.

All minutes to be numbered in consecutive order. Continue on other side if necessary

14

At a point several hundred yards into the mire searchers discovered an area of firm ground with vaulted rocks and a pit. In the base of the pit were countless animal bones, no doubt the remains of sheep taken from the moor to feed the hound as this was clearly the lair at which is was kept.

Traces of the phosphor preparation were also discovered, but still no trace of Mr Stapleton who all believe has been lost to the mire, although in such circumstances, there is no evidence, and he may yet be found to have made good his escape.

I understand this fellow may yet be subject to further investigation regarding other serious crimes within the jurisdiction of the Devon County Constabulary.

This officer returned to London the following day, 19th October having met with Detective Superintendent Johns of the Devon County Constabulary.

Respectfully Submitted


G Lestrade
G. Lestrade
Detective Inspector 704
Criminal Investigation Department
Scotland Yard

All minutes to be numbered in consecutive order. Continue on other side if necessary

15

(2)

Detective Chief Superintendent

I beg to report that having read Detective Superintendent Johns report I can find no valid reason as to why this Mr Holmes could simply not have enlisted the assistance of officers from the Devon County Constabulary to assist him apprehend the suspect Stapleton.

Perhaps a larger number of officers deployed to the vicinity of Merripits House would have resulted in the successful apprehension of Mr Baskerville rather than the unsatisfactory situation that Devon County Constabulary find themselves in now, where the death of the suspect is only presumed rather than confirmed.

Detective Inspector Lestrade has been tasked with obtaining a full statement of facts from Mr Holmes and Dr. Watson for the information of Detective Superintendent Johns.

I have spoken with the officer regarding any future requests for the assistance of this office from Mrs Holmes and how unlikely we are to look upon them with favour.

Submitted

M Kellenson
Detective Chief Inspector
Criminal Investigation Department
Scotland Yard

All minutes to be numbered in consecutive order. Continue on other side if necessary

(*3*)

In my view this entire episode has been nothing more than a staggering waste of Metropolitan Police resources. I take a very dim view of Scotland Yard officers being deployed simply to enhance the reputation of this fellow Holmes.

Be kind enough to arrange a meeting with Mr Holmes in my office at his earliest convenience. I think a frank discussion is in order.

R Steel

Detective Chief Superintendent

Criminal Investigation Department

Scotland Yard

All minutes to be numbered in consecutive order. Continue on other side if necessary

17

# Devon County Constabulary

Borough - *Totnes*

Station - *Buckfastleigh*

Date - *Monday 1ˢᵗ November 1889*

Reference - *DCC 1435 / 89*

Reporting Officer - *Detective Superintendent Johns*

**REPORT -**

*Chief Constable*

*I pray to report upon events occurring within this Totnes Borough on dates between Saturday 4ᵗʰ May 1889 and Saturday 18ᵗʰ October 1889.*

*1.       On the night of Saturday 4ᵗʰ May 1889 at approximately 12pm, a Mr John Barrymore the domestic manservant at Baskerville Hall in the parish of Grimpen, discovered the apparently lifeless body of Sir Charles Baskerville (Born 16. 02. 1843).*

2.	The body was lying face down on a gravel pathway some 50 yds from a wicket gate at the boundary of the Baskerville Hall Estate. The pathway is bordered with an avenue of yew trees and extends the full length of 150 yds from the Hall, past the picket gate and beyond to a pavilion. The gate in question was locked.

3.	Mr Barrymore states that he became concerned for the welfare of his master after he discovered the main door to Baskerville Hall open and his master still absent at a particularly late hour.

4.	Mr Barrymore equipped himself with a storm lantern and traversed Baskerville Hall until reaching the avenue of ornamental yew trees, the usual route for his master's walk.

5. The entire day had been damp and Sir Charles' footprints were easily to distinguish upon the gravel pathway. Some 50yds beyond the picket gateway, Barrymore discovered the body of his master.

6. On approaching the body, not knowing if there was life still in Sir Charles, Mr Barrymore reported no sign of any mortal injury but observed the most horrific contortions upon his master's face. Barrymore immediately determined that nothing could be done and retreated to the Hall and despatched the estate groom, Joshua Perkins, to make speed to nearby Meldon House and summon to the scene Dr Mortimer, a friend of Sir Charles and a respected local physician.

7.	Dr Mortimer arrived at Baskerville Hall by his own carriage at 01.05hrs and examined the body of Sir Charles and pronounced life extinct. Dr. Mortimer could not at that stage determine any likely cause of death but he too remarks upon the grotesque contortions upon the face of Sir Charles, describing them as so terrible as to almost make him completely unrecognisable to his friend.

8.	In response to a request from Dr Mortimer, police were called to Baskerville Hall and, at 03.40hrs on Sunday 5th May; Police Sergeant 5 Brigg attended having ridden by horse from Buckfastleigh Police Station. Upon his arrival he examined the body of Sir Charles which had been removed from the gravel path by Dr Mortimer and Mr Barrymore into the boot room at Baskerville Hall where it was lain on the floor, on its back and covered with a linen bed sheet.

9.    Having questioned Dr Mortimer and Mr Barrymore as to the events that evening, PS Brigg examined the corpse and noted that rigour-mortis was not yet present. There were marks upon the face and hands thought consistent with grazing from a fall. Also present were fresh scuff marks upon the knees of Sir Charles' tweed breeches and scrapes to the polished toe-caps of his boots, again consistent with a forwards fall onto a gravel surface.

10.    Due to the late hour it was agreed that the body of Sir Charles would be removed the following day and the corpse was left in the boot room at Baskerville Hall and PS Brigg and Doctor Mortimer departed.

11.     At 08.45hrs, Police Contstables 441 Waering and 580 Cash arrived with the Coroner's carriage. Dr Mortimer had returned to Baskerville Hall and identified the mortal remains of Sir Charles to PC Waering, whereupon the officers removed the body by carriage to the Tavistock Mortuary where the remains were identified by Pc Waering to the Coroner's assistant, Mr Sharp.

12.     A post-mortem examination conducted at Tavistock Mortuary on Monday 6th May by Professor Kennedy (Frcp) determined that Sir Charles Baskerville died a natural death caused by congestion of the heart, an ailment that had been upon him for some months if not years.

13.	An inquest was opened on Friday 10th May by H.M. Coroner in Tavistock Coroners Court and on hearing the available evidence was closed that very same day with the finding that Sir Charles Baskerville died from natural causes. His body was released to Doctor Mortimer for Christian burial and has since been interred at a private location on the Baskerville Hall Estate

14.	The Inquest verdict did much to quell the notion circulating amidst local folk, on Dartmoor in particular, that the demise of Sir Charles Baskerville was the result of some blight or terrible curse on the Baskerville family involving some hound or beast that set upon him from the moor.

15.     The same can be said for a piece in the Devon County Chronicle dated 14th May in which the facts of the case were published in great detail for public consumption.

16.     By universal agreement, and in association with Messrs. Hall, Cartwright and Co Solicitors, Sir Charles' legal representatives in Exeter, Doctor Mortimer was appointed the executor of Sir Charles' will.

17.     Having exhausted all other avenues of enquiry, Doctor Mortimer identified a Sir Henry Baskerville as being the rightful heir to the estate. His enquiries led him to believe that the baronet was living in the United States of America.

18.    On 10th June 1889 Doctor Mortimer wrote to the Pinkerton National Detective Agency in New York to engage their services in the search for Sir Henry Baskerville and on 12th July a telegram was received to indicate that they had traced a gentleman of those particulars to the region of New Brunswick in South-Eastern Canada. This was confirmed by letter to Doctor Mortimer on 14th July.

19.    Further enquiries by Pinkertons confirm that Sir Henry Baskerville is indeed the rightful heir to the estate and on 30th July Sir Henry Baskerville himself corresponds direct with Doctor Mortimer to express his intention to arrange passage to England to view the Baskerville Hall estate.

20. On 24th September Sir Henry Baskerville departed New York aboard the American Lines vessel, the S.S.St. Louis, bound to arrive at the port of Southampton on 30th September. Upon disembarking the vessel, arrangements were in hand for rail travel to Waterloo and for Sir Henry Baskerville to take a suite at the Northumberland Hotel on Northumberland Avenue.

21. On the afternoon of 30th September, Doctor Mortimer held a consultation with Mr Sherlock Holmes, the renowned criminal investigator, at his rooms at 221b, Baker Street in London. Also present at this meeting was an associate of Mr Holmes, a Doctor Watson who also resides at 221b Baker Street.

22. In the course of this consultation it appears that Doctor Mortimer introduces Mr Holmes to the local tale surrounding the Baskerville family and the supposed curse upon the line and dangers of the hound from upon the moor.

23. This is of significant relevance to this Constabulary's enquiries into the circumstances surrounding the death of Sir Charles Baskerville in that Doctor Mortimer suggests to Mr Holmes that, contrary to his written statement of $7^{th}$ May and his sworn evidence to H. M. Coroner on $10^{th}$ May, he saw other footmarks in the vicinity of the body of Sir Charles as he lay dead upon the gravel path at Baskerville Hall on $4^{th}$ May.

24. Doctor Mortimer suggests to Mr Holmes that some little distance off from the body, but fresh and clear, were visible the footprints of a gigantic hound. This revelation is at complete odds with his original recollections.

25. By these disclosures Doctor Mortimer makes plain that he gives some credence to the notion that Sir Charles died that night of fear from an encounter with such a hound.

26. Doctor Mortimer appears to have conducted enquiries within the parish and to have discovered others who claim sightings of such a beast. Our own enquiries reveal nothing but myth and legend regarding such matters. Certainly over time there have been incidents upon the moor involving feral beasts and the savaging of livestock but certainly nothing to merit the notion that some hound is about the moor.

27. Regardless, Doctor Mortimer appears sufficiently concerned of what he learns to seek advice from Mr Holmes as to what best to do with Sir Henry Baskerville who was due to arrive in London that very day. In seeking to convince Mr Holmes as to the existence of the hound he appears bent on creating the notion that there is some similar risk to the person of Sir Henry should he venture as planned to Baskerville Hall.

28. I find it incredulous that Mr Holmes appears to indulge Doctor Mortimer to the extent that a further meeting was arranged for 1$^{st}$ October at which it was suggested Sir Henry himself should be present. Doctor Mortimer was despatched to greet Sir Henry and escort him to his suite at the Northumberland Hotel.

29.	On waking on the morning of 1st October, Sir Henry was confronted by two oddities, the first, that one of his newly acquired boots had been mislaid from outside his room where it had been left for polishing, the second was a letter addressed to him at the hotel when none but he and Doctor Mortimer knew of his address in London.

30.	The letter was postmarked from the evening before, having been posted in Charing Cross in London. The letter itself was a single sheet of writing paper onto which separate words from newsprint had been cut and glued to form a sentence.

31.	The page read – 'As you value your life or your reason, keep away from the moor'. The word moor was written by hand in ink, the remainder, Mr Holmes deduced,    were cut from the Times newspaper, and cut with nail scissors at that.

32. Doctor Mortimer now imparts what appears to pass between them as fact to Sir Henry, resulting in agreement that the consultation should end but reconvene at 2pm at the Northumberland Hotel for luncheon.

33. Sir Henry and Doctor Mortimer then leave Baker Street to walk to their hotel, however unbeknownst to them, are kept under close surveillance by Mr. Holmes and Doctor Watson, also on foot. After only a short distance Mr Holmes becomes aware of a hansom cab which he believes is shadowing Doctor Mortimer and Sir Henry.

34. On approaching the cab Holmes catches the most fleeting of glimpses of a male passenger sporting a full black beard (a feature that Mr Holmes believes immediately to be false) before the cab is instructed to make off and is lost to sight.

35.    Despite the confusion of the moment Mr Holmes was able to make a record of the number of the hansom cab as No.2704 and subsequently undertook enquiries with the Official Registry of the London Carriage Office to determine the identity of the badge holder and through him, the identity of his passenger.

36.    Mr Holmes then solicited the services of a young messenger boy named Cartwright and provided him with a list of hotels to visit within the area with a view to securing access to their discarded paper-waste, looking in particular to locate the centre pages from the Times newspaper of the previous day from which the note to Sir Henry was cut, and thus locate the hotel at which the sender was staying.

37. On arrival at the Northumberland Hotel, Mr Holmes made discreet enquires that satisfied his concerns that the letter writer was not indeed rooming there.

38. On meeting Sir Henry it was revealed that another of his boots had gone astray, this time one of a well-worn and favoured pair, and still no sign of the original missing new brown boot. Despite his evident agitation at such incompetence, Sir Henry appeared to be sufficiently focused upon the purpose of their meeting to resolve to take up residence at Baskerville Hall.

39. During this luncheon Doctor Mortimer disclosed to Sir Henry and the assembled company that the Baskerville Estate held value in the region of one million pounds

40.  Doctor Mortimer also reveals that he was the recipient of a bequest in the sum of one thousand pounds from Sir Charles' will as were the Barrymores, the domestic help who each received five hundred pounds. This appears to have interested Mr Holmes as much as the discovery that John Barrymore wears a full beard.

41.  The gentlemen determine to discover whether it was Mr Barrymore who was following Sir Henry as the passenger in the hansom cab or was he, as he ought to be, at Baskerville Hall preparing for the arrival of Sir Henry. Mr Holmes conceived a plan that while simple would alert them to the truth that very same evening. This of course presupposes that Mr Holmes has it in mind at this stage that Barrymore is in some way responsible for the note to Sir Henry, knowing as only very few might, the travel plans of Doctor Mortimer.

42.     It was agreed that two telegrams would be sent to Devonshire from London. The first would be delivered to Barrymore himself enquiring in general terms if arrangements were progressing satisfactorily, it would by its nature require an immediate reply should he be there to provide it. The second would require the postmaster at Grimpen to deliver it to Barrymore, but should he not be there to receive it, send word directly to the Northumberland Hotel.

43.     As a plan it held obvious merit, however, unfortunately for Mr Holmes his suspicions proved unfounded as by evening word was received that Mr Barrymore was indeed at Baskerville Hall. Mr Holmes faired no better in his search for the mutilated newspaper as searches by his young agent failed to discover anything of note.

44. The only thing of benefit to come from this luncheon appears to be the discovery of the missing tan boot in the very private room in which they took their meal. Doctor Mortimer and Sir Henry both professed to have searched the room beforehand and found nothing and suspicions that the German waiter who served on them at table may have returned the item proved fruitless.

45. Another point had been discussed in the course of the meal, and this came from Mr Holmes himself. It was agreed that his associate Dr Watson would accompany Sir Henry to Baskerville Hall as it was considered that Doctor Mortimer would be distracted by the demands of his medical practice upon his return to Grimpen.

46.    The following day, arrangements were made for the party to travel by rail from Paddington Station to Buckfastleigh, departing on Saturday 4th October at 10.30am

47.    By late evening Holmes had the name of the driver of the hansom cab seen earlier in the day. Having been informed of the request for his particulars, and being somewhat curious as to the interest in him, the driver presented himself at Mr Holmes' rooms to be interviewed regarding events only to disappoint by the revelation that his fare had alighted from the cab at Waterloo Station and had pleasure in advising the driver that he had that day driven the famous detective Sherlock Holmes.

48.    At almost that very same late hour, one Arthur George Selden (CRO-14184/81G) - Prisoner Number 1882D, made good his escape from Dartmoor Prison at Princetown, On 28th August 1888 Selden had been found guilty at the Central Criminal Court on two counts of murder, been sentenced to hang until dead but had his sentence repealed to life imprisonment after the court accepted submissions as to his mental health.


49.    On alighting from the train at Buckfastleigh, the party from London would have immediately seen evidence of large numbers of Constables and Prison Guards about the moor.

50. On arrival at Baskerville Hall Sir Henry and Doctor Watson were greeted by Mr and Mrs Barrymore while Doctor Mortimer bade his leave and continued by carriage to his home at Meldon House in Grimpen to be reunited with his wife.

51. Doctor Watson reports upon a quiet evening spent dining and in conversation with Sir Henry and of some time spent adjusting to the sounds of the moor before retiring early to bed. He had in his possession his service revolver (Doctor Watson was in possession of a current licence in accordance with the Gun Licence Act 1870) and I am instructed that he is an excellent shot having seen service in Afghan with the 5th Northumberland Fusiliers

52.	One sound in the night that did concern Doctor Watson was the noise of a woman sobbing, a matter he raised with Sir Henry over breakfast. Mr Barrymore was questioned regarding the sound and he stated that he knew it had not been his wife, one of only two women in the house at that particular hour.

53.	Doctor Watson saw Mrs Barrymore in the morning before breakfast was served and noticed that her eyes were bloodshot and gave every appearance of her having been crying. It would be fair to say that at this stage, Doctor Watson was forming deeper suspicions regarding Mr Barrymore to the point where he resolved to visit Grimpen Post Office to confirm whether the telegrams had been delivered exactly as Mr Holmes had specified.

54. Taking his leave of Sir Henry, Doctor Watson made the four mile journey on foot to Grimpen Post Office where he spoke with the Postmaster, Mr Edward Wright. He disclosed that his son, James, had delivered the telegram to Baskerville Hall. On questioning the lad it was discovered that, contrary to instructions, the telegram had been delivered into the hand of Mrs Barrymore, she claiming that her husband, unseen by the lad, was working in the loft and unable to come down when his wife was on hand to take delivery of it.

55. I have a thought here that Mr Holmes may have been too clever for his own good in this regard, expecting moorland folk to appreciate the subtleties of his devices.

56.   As Doctor Watson made his way back from Grimpen he was met by Mr Jack Stapleton, a friend of Doctor Mortimer. Mr Stapleton expressed a keen knowledge of the work of Mr Holmes and Doctor Watson and was overtly curious as to Sir Henry's view of the superstitions concerning the hound. Stapleton disclosed some knowledge of Sir Charles' ill health and seemed to share with Doctor Mortimer the belief that a hound as featured in these tales had caused the death.

57.   Whether Doctor Watson expressed the sentiment, or whether it was discernable from his demeanour, but Mr Stapleton appears to have realised that he might have been somewhat too direct in his manner, something for which he tries to make immediate amends by inviting Doctor Watson to his home, Merripits House to meet his sister.

58.	After only a short distance after diverting along the path to Merripits House Doctor Watson reports hearing a deep roar that rose and fell from some distance away. Mr Stapleton assured Doctor Watson that it was most likely to be the sound of a Bittern booming from the great Grimpen Mire off to their north. Doctor Watson states that the sound was not that of a bird of any kind.

59.	Mr Stapleton directed Doctor Watson's attention to the dangers of the expanse of Grimpen Mire that surrounded them, but no sooner had he done so that he ran off onto the treacherous mire, apparently in pursuit of some rare butterfly leaving Doctor Watson alone on the path.

60.    No sooner did he find himself alone when Doctor Watson became aware of the approach of a young woman from the direction of Merripits House. He was about to make his introduction when the lady spoke and in hushed and hurried tones and as much as implored him to 'go back' and 'leave the moor for London immediately'.

61.    It was clearly intended as a warning, and certainly not intended to be overheard by Mr Stapleton, for as he returned to their view the lady promptly changed the subject. She introduced herself to Doctor Watson as being Stapleton's sister. Watson could not help but notice the stark contrast in their looks, he fair skinned, she almost Latin in appearance.

62.  Doctor Watson makes it clear from his reports that as Stapleton returned to their company the atmosphere between Mr Stapleton and his sister was most strained, to say the least, and after Doctor Watson had identified himself by way of introduction, it became immediately obvious from her expression that when the young lady had addressed those warnings to Doctor Watson, she had done so in the mistaken belief that she was actually addressing Sir Henry.

63.  Uneasy in this company, Doctor Watson made his excuses and returned along the path from whence he came only to encounter Miss Stapleton further along the path at which point she made feeble attempts to mitigate her previous remarks.

64.   One other issue of concern remained in Doctor Watson's thoughts, is that of the criminal Selden, still at large on the moor. Despite his misgivings about the pair from his initial encounter, his concerns appear to extend to the Stapleton household and in later discussions with Sir Henry, consideration was given to having Perkins, the groom, sleep at Merripits House to afford the Stapletons some added security, but Stapleton himself would hear nothing of it.

65.   It would be fair to say that in the two weeks following Selden's escape, there was little hope given to his survival as an intensive search of the moor had revealed nothing of him, nor sign of fire or slaughter for sustenance. Many believed him to have perished in the cold or in the mires.

66.    In the days after his arrival Sir Henry makes the acquaintance of his neighbours and travels freely about the parishes in the company of the ever-watchful Doctor Watson who corresponds with Mr Holmes in some detail upon events, as uneventful as they may be.

67.    It would appear that Doctor Watson had been instructed on leaving London by Mr Holmes to acquaint himself with as many folk about the area as possible and to use his skills to determine their bona-fides.    This done, I am convinced that suspicion still fell on Mr Barrymore, for being in some way involved in issuing the warning letter and the hansom cab pursuit of Sir Henry in London.

68.     Sir Henry appears to be inclined to this view also, so much so that on 14th October Sir Henry and Doctor Watson conduct and interview of him to determine his exact whereabouts and movements at the time young James Thomas delivered Holmes' telegram to Baskerville Hall. Barrymore confirmed that he had not received the telegram, nor did he pen the reply as he was busy in the box-room. He claims to have had the message read to him by his wife and to have directed her as to what should be sent in reply.

69.     That evening, Sir Henry detects that Barrymore is concerned that he has in some way incurred his master's ire and so seeks to mollify his manservant with the gift of some of his London clothing purchases, his own effects having arrived from Canada.

70.    Later still, having retired to bed, Watson, a self professed light sleeper, was roused by the noise of footsteps passing the corridor outside his room. On investigating, he makes out the form of Mr Barrymore edging along the passageway and entering one of the unfurnished guest rooms where he is seen to stand motionless with a candle at the window. Watson was able to remain unobserved throughout the episode and in the morning visits the room in question and by standing at the window determines that it, of all on the west face of the Hall, provides the clearest view of the moor. Watson discusses these events with Sir Henry over breakfast only to discover that he too has heard Barrymore about in the night and always at about the same hour. A plan is hatched to observe Barrymore at night.

71. Following breakfast, Sir Henry dressed as if to leave the Hall on foot and as instructed by Holmes, Doctor Watson dresses quickly to accompany him on his walk. Sir Henry, though is quick to thwart Watson in his plan and reveals something to Watson, something that he himself had already noted developing, namely a growing affection in the relationship between Sir Henry and Mr Stapleton's sister on whom Sir Henry has taken occasion to call with increasing regularity.

72. With some candour Sir Henry also revealed that he was troubled by the prospect that this burgeoning relationship apparently did not entirely meet with the approval of Mr Stapleton himself.

73. Sir Henry left Baskerville Hall, but was followed at a discreet distance by Doctor Watson who felt bound by his oath to accompany Sir Henry at all times, especially should he venture onto the moor. A short time into his surveillance he observed Sir Henry in the company of Miss Stapleton.

74. The two were seen in animated discussion at almost the very same spot on the moor path where Doctor Watson has first encountered Miss Stapleton. His elevated position allowed him to observe that, rather than being alone, the couple were about to be discovered by none other than Mr Stapleton himself. Doctor Watson observed the very moment of their discovery and noted the extremely agitated manner in which Stapleton reacted, apparently remonstrating quite firmly with Sir Henry.

75.	Their exchange concluded only when Stapleton as much as directed his sister return back the way she had first arrived. Sir Henry departed the spot himself in a much agitated state and after a short distance Doctor Watson broke cover from the hillside and appeared upon the path to Sir Henry who professed his profound bemusement that Stapleton should object to so fine a suitor for his sister.

76.	That evening Sir Henry and Doctor Watson struck a plan to resolve the mystery surrounding Barrymore's furtive movements about the house. Both men took dinner before retiring as usual, but then Doctor Watson joined Sir Henry in his rooms, in silence, in the dark, until beyond the hour of 3am, all to no avail as not a sound was heard.

77. The following evening, 15th October, the plan was repeated, again with both men taking station in Sir Henry's rooms. The hours passed until just after 2am when the sound of footsteps passed outside the door. Sir Henry and Doctor Watson waited a brief moment then followed Barrymore into the same vacant room and found him at the window with a candle.

78. Doctor Watson was quick to deduce that the movement of the candle was a signal to someone outside at some point yonder on the moor. True enough it seems, as when they peered off into the darkness they could make out a light emanating from the region of Cleft Tor, a mile or so distant from the Hall.

79.    Sir Henry challenged Barrymore for the truth and the identity of who it might be signalling out on the moor but he responded with only impertinent evasiveness to the point where Sir Henry had no option but to dismiss him on the spot and threaten to eject his family in dishonour from the Hall. Still there was no word from Barrymore and the situation was only recovered when his wife Eliza appeared in the room.

80.    Despite her husband's protestations she revealed that the movement of the candle was a prearranged signal to her brother who was at large on the moor, and that he was none other than Arthur Selden, the escaped convict, the Notting Hill murderer.

81.	Mrs Barrymore revealed that she and her husband had no knowledge of the escape but had provided sanctuary for him at Baskerville Hall for one night following his escape. In her regular correspondence to him in prison she had unwittingly provided sufficient information concerning the location of Baskerville Hall for him to find it following his escape. After his first night the telegram arrived from Mr Holmes indicating the impending arrival of Sir Henry at the Hall and this had throw their arrangement into disarray and Selden had been forced to retreat from the Hall and conceal himself about the moor. He had been delivered provisions each second night, the signal from the Hall being the sign that food was available, the response from the moor indicated the location at which he could be found waiting.

82. Sir Henry and Doctor Watson decided to chase onto the moor and apprehend Selden. As they neared the source of the light they heard the most fearsome sound, a roar that rose and fell, the very same sound Doctor Watson had heard before near Meritpits House.

83. A candle was seen wedged between some rocks but there was no sign of Selden. The felon then broke cover and made to run from the spot, throwing rocks at Sir Henry and Doctor Watson to deter them. Selden's familiarity with the terrain proved to be his advantage and in no time the distance between them was too great and the chase was up. Just then, Doctor Watson glimpsed the form of another man, high upon a tor, against the moonlight.

84.  In the moment it took Watson to point the fellow out to Sir Henry, the moon had passed and the figure had disappeared. Convinced it was a prison guard about their search, Sir Henry, (apparently deeply unnerved by the earlier sound), suggests that they return to Baskerville Hall rather than continue their pursuit. On their return they retire immediately to bed.

85.  Quite understandably the mood that morning is reported as melancholy, made worse by an exchange between Sir Henry and Mr Barrymore during the course of which Barrymore has the temerity to rebuke Sir Charles for acting upon Mrs Barrymore's admissions and giving chase to Selden.

86. As will be seen from Mr Barrymore's more recent statement, not only were he and his wife providing shelter and sustenance to an escaped felon, they were privy to his plans to imminently escape these shores and steal passage to South America and my officers will be investigating these matters and I hope to be in a position to report further in due course.

87. At some point in the conversation that morning an accommodation appears to have been reached to effectively allow Selden his freedom by not reporting the matter to the appropriate authorities, something which had we not been overtaken by events, and regardless of the stature of the individuals involved, I would wish to have seen subject to a full criminal investigation.

88. To continue. In what I believe to be in exchange for Selden's freedom, Barrymore then revealed that on the morning of the 4th May, the day he met his death, Sir Charles had received a letter in a women's hand asking him to be at the picket gate at 10 o'clock and to burn the letter after reading it. The letter was signed only with the letters L.L. and was postmarked Coombe Tracey.

89. This information came only from Mr Barrymore's recollections as he states that Mrs Barrymore had found only that charred portion in the grate in the weeks after Sir Charles's death. The remnant did not itself survive and so we have no physical evidence in support of what Barrymore claims.

90.     My own investigations reveal that the post was delivered to Baskerville Hall that day at 11.55hrs, at or around the usual hour. A letter posted in Coombe Tracey on one day, would certainly be expected to reach the hand of the intended recipient by the next at around noon. From that we can be entirely confident that the sender of the letter was seeking a meeting at 10pm, not 10am. As we know from Barrymore's original statement, and from the evidence of others, Sir Charles was a man of habit and one thing is of interest here in particular, his fashion for walking at the hour of 10pm each night. Moreover, his regular walk took him past the picket gate by the yew avenue where Doctor Mortimer discovered cigar ash the night Sir Charles died.

91.    Later that evening and without reference to Sir Charles, Doctor Watson set off from the Hall to the spot where he had seen the stranger during the chase for Selden. The search proved fruitless, however, on walking back to Baskerville Hall Doctor Watson had a fortunate chance encounter with Doctor Mortimer who was about the moor in his trap in search of his Spaniel.

92.    Having accepted a lift, and without troubling Doctor Mortimer with the reasons behind the enquiry, Doctor Watson asked if any females within these parishes could be identified by the moniker 'L.L.', those as appeared upon the letter to Sir Charles. Doctor Mortimer suggested that Miss Lucy Lyons, a local resident, Mr Frankland's daughter, might fit the bill adding that she was resident in Coombe Tracey.

93.   On returning with Doctor Watson to Baskerville Hall Doctor Mortimer was invited for lunch by Sir Henry. For his part, Doctor Watson does not act upon this new information but reports the news instead to Mr Holmes whom I fancy he hoped to lure to Devonshire, such was the pace of developments.

94.   After dinner, Sir Henry and Doctor Mortimer entertained themselves with cards and so provided Doctor Watson the opportunity to question Barrymore once more. During the interview Watson discovers that Selden himself had reported sightings of a stranger on the moor. This stranger had apparently enlisted assistance from Coombe Tracey for the delivery of provisions and other wants and was himself hidden about the moor.

95.    On the morning of 18<sup>th</sup> October, having heard nothing in reply from Mr Holmes, Doctor Watson was taken by Perkins the groom to interview Miss Lyons in Coombe Tracey.

96.    In interview Miss Lyons admits to corresponding twice with Sir Charles with a view to express her gratitude for financial assistance. Without detailing much of a delicate matter, Miss Lyons stated that Mr Stapleton had informed Sir Charles of her plight and that is how they had come to correspond. Miss Lyons though, vehemently denied corresponding with Sir Charles on 4<sup>th</sup> May, that is until Doctor Watson recited the passage obtained from the scorched fragment in the study grate.

97.    The revelation clearly distressed Miss Lyons, however, she appears to have recovered her composure sufficiently to explain to Doctor Watson that she had requested the meeting upon hearing that Sir Charles would be leaving Baskerville Hall the very next day for an indefinite stay in London. Miss Lyons saw this as the last opportunity to seek his assistance on a matter of some delicacy.

98.    The lateness of the hour and the specific location, away from the house, were designed to protect her modesty. Pressed as to the outcome of a meeting just prior to his death Miss Lyons would only state that a most private affair had preventing her from attending at all.

99. When pressed by Doctor Watson as the matter concerned Miss Lyons suggested her reasons for requesting a meeting with Sir Charles were no deeper than to implore him for financial assistance in settling legal fees that would finance a divorce, and see her rid once and for all of her estranged husband, A rapprochement with her father was not possible after he had disowned her for marrying without his permission and Sir Charles was, in desperation, the last resort.

100. That said, Miss Lyons explained the need to meet Sir Charles was made redundant when she received help from another party and so she did not keep the meeting as had been arranged in the letter.

101.    On leaving Miss Lyons, and with the investigation taken no further, Doctor Watson decided to search once more for the stranger on the moor. Had it not been for the waiting Perkins he would have set off at once but good fortune came his way with an approach from none other than Mr Frankland, Miss Lyons father, who invited Doctor Watson to share news of good fortune over a glass of wine.

102.    This fortunate intervention provided Doctor Watson the opportunity to release Perkins with the intention of resuming his search once he had finished at Mr Frankland's house

103.    Mr Frankland is a gentleman well known to police, not for any criminality, but from his involvement with the courts as a serial litigant. A man learned in the law, Mr Frankland taxes the capacity of courts, high and low, on a frequent basis. The outcomes of these cases can at times endear him to local folk and at others set the same community against him with equal passion as sometimes requires a considerable number of constables to keep the peace in Coombe Tracey.

104.    Once in Frankland's parlour, in the euphoria following a win in the courts, and after a glass of wine he confides in Watson that he has some inkling as to the possible whereabouts of the convict Selden upon the moor.

105. He shows Doctor Watson a telescope which is trained upon the skyline at Black Tor, the very spot where Doctor Watson had spied his mysterious stranger. Mr Falkland reveals that on several occasions, at regular times of day, he has spied a boy ferrying a bundle to a particular spot.

106. As he tells his tale to Doctor Watson he peers through the telescope and doesn't that very thing happen, and through the glass the form of the boy is seen furtively moving along the skyline, bundle in hand. Doctor Watson himself peers through the glass to se the form of the young lad moving across the rocky terrain. Immediately Doctor Watson set off on foot.

107.	At sunset, Doctor Watson reached the spot where he judged he had last seen the boy, an outcrop beneath Black Tor which afforded him a view into the shallow valley below from where he could make out several settlement huts, only one of which seemed the most likely to afford any shelter.

108.	Doctor Watson drew his revolver and approached the hut only to find nobody within. On searching about the small hut he discovered a scribbled note outlining his visit that day to Coombe Tracey, some laundry including several gentlemen's collars and some bedding. Doctor Watson concedes the sudden fear that it is he, not Sir Henry who is under observation from the stranger.

109.   At that very moment the stranger returns, only for Watson to discover that it is no other than Mr Sherlock Holmes who has been observing events unfold for himself from a distance so as not to alert or unnerve Doctor Watson or those concerned in the whole affair. Young Cartwright, an express delivery boy who had been employed by Holmes to search about the hotels for the mutilated Times newspaper, had been brought down from London and pressed into delivering food and essentials to Holmes together with Watson's reports which had been redirected from Baker Street.

110.   Cartwright was also relaying snippets of information to Holmes regarding what was known of the movements of all concerned and it would appear that Holmes was as well versed with the case as his associate.

111.	Doctor Watson was debriefed by Holmes who disclosed that his own enquiries revealed Stapleton and his sister to be actually man and wife. Moreover, Holmes added to the confusion of the moment by suggesting to Doctor Watson that he had discovered evidence of some intimacy between Stapleton and Miss Lyons.

112.	Holmes had made antecedent enquiries of Stapleton from his time as schoolmaster in Yorkshire. Those enquiries had led him to the discovery that the owner of the school had fled with his wife, and not only did the physical descriptions of the pair tally, but the missing schoolmaster was an ardent entomologist, as was Stapleton. The infatuation with Miss Lyons remained unexplained but Holmes and Watson agreed that she should first learn of his deception from them in the hope that she would provide valuable evidence in turn against him.

113.    It was further agreed that Holmes would remain at a distance upon the moor for another 48 hours and that Doctor Watson should return to the care of his charge at Baskerville Hall.

114.    At that very instant an ungodly sound was upon them from the distance, as wretched a human sound as ever heard. Above it, the now unmistakeable noise of the hound. Both men raced in the direction of the sound, stopping at intervals to locate the source. On a downward slope, at the edge of a precipice amidst rubble and boulders they came upon the contorted body of a man. The neck was broken and the skull was crushed and blood haemorrhaged from the wound, there was no sign of life.

115.    By the light of a match the body was thought initially to be that of Sir Henry, dressed as it was in Sir Henry's familiar tweed clothes, the very garments he had worn when at Baker Street. As Holmes and Doctor Watson moved the body to remove the corpse to Baskerville Hall they discovered that it was in fact the convict Selden, dressed in Sir Henry's clothes. The circumstances suggested that, chased by the hound, Selden fell from the path to his death.

116.    While Watson and Holmes pondered what to do with Selden's body, they were joined from the darkness by none other than Stapleton. He too believed the dead man to be Sir Henry, particularly as he had invited him to dine at Merripits House that evening and he not yet appeared.

117. The long trek to Baskerville Hall allows Holmes and Watson time to reflect upon their case and how, in truth they had none. Stapleton was a man who figured in their suspicions of foul play but then had not Barrymore. On legends and suppositions tales for magazines are plotted, cases for the courts are not fashioned in such a manner.

118. That evening Mr Holmes ate supper with Sir Henry and apprised him of such facts as he thought palatable and necessary. During their discussions Holmes appears to be distracted by the many family portraits that hung around the hall. That of Sir Hugo Baskerville, he who was the source of legend regarding the hounds, held a particular fascination for Holmes.

119.    After Sir Henry retired, Holmes returned to the salon with Doctor Watson and by masking all but the facial features of Sir Hugo on the portrait was able to solve the case at one fell swoop. I have seen this done for my own benefit and in truth it is remarkable, the facial features on the portrait are identical to those of Stapleton, who was in truth a Baskerville descendent.

120.    It transpired the following morning that Sir Henry had plans to dine with Stapleton that evening. Holmes gave word to Sir Henry that both he and Watson were bound for London, news he was determined would reach Stapleton. That same morning I received notification by runner that the Dartmoor Prison authorities had been advised of the location of Selden's body, the message sent by Mr Holmes included detailed information as to the manner of his death.

121.     I gave instructions for his remains to be transported back to prison, where, after formal identification by Mr Barrymore and a post-mortem examination confirmed death as a consequence of a cranial fracture and broken neck, he was interred within the walls. I confess to some satisfaction that this vile felon met his end by a broken neck, if not at the end of a rope upon the scaffold, then by some other means.

122.     As regards Sir Henry's dinner appointment at Merripits House, Holmes gave strict instructions that he was to arrive by carriage but send it back stating his intention to return back across the moor on foot. Holmes and Watson make their farewells and then set off for Coombe Tracey railway station by trap.

123. Once Perkins has left the station Holmes met with his young aide Cartwright who was instructed to take the train to London and upon arrival send a wire in the name of Sherlock Holmes to Sir Henry at Baskerville Hall, thus completing the illusion that both men were no longer about the area. A message for Holmes at the Station Office confirmed the later arrival of Detective Inspector Lestrade from Scotland Yard who had been summoned by telegram.

124. Mr Holmes and Doctor Watson called on Miss Lyons and outlined to her the fact that Stapleton was already married and produced documentary evidence, including photographs of the couple, in the identity of Mr and Mrs Vandeleur.

125. Miss Lyons turned in an instant against her bigamous suitor and admitted what she knew to Holmes and Watson. She stated that it was a letter of his dictation that she had sent to Sir Charles requesting the meeting at the picket gate at 10pm on 4th May. Further, having posted that very same letter, it was Stapleton who then promised to fund the divorce himself and dissuaded her from keeping the appointment.

126. On subsequently hearing of the death of Sir Charles she was persuaded to keep her tongue by Stapleton who instilled a fear in her that she may be thought complicit in his demise, and so perhaps arrested and further shame and misery brought to her father.

127.  On leaving Miss Lyons they left her rooms and returned to the railway station to meet the 17.05 London Express, and with it, Detective Inspector Lestrade of whose arrival, I regret to say, we did not receive even the courtesy of a mention as is customary, something I trust we shall be taking up with Scotland Yard in the near future.

128.  After dining close by, and under the cover of darkness, the three men made their way on foot to within 200 yds of Merripits House with the kitchen windows closest to their view. Doctor Watson ventured forward to just beyond the boundary wall, a vantage point that allowed an easy view into the dining room where he had a clear view of Sir Henry and Stapleton together.

129.    After just a moment Stapleton disappeared from view only to emerge from the house and visit an adjacent out-house, only a short distance from Watson's position. His visit was accompanied by a noise from within, the exact origin Watson could not determine. After only a minute Stapleton returned to the house into the company of Sir Henry.

130.    Stapleton's wife was nowhere to be seen and at just after 10pm the servants dimmed the kitchen light leaving the two men in the dining room. A thick blanket of fog was fast threatening to engulf the house and the trio retreated half a mile from the house to keep ahead of the fog and on taking their positions were rewarded with the sound of boots approaching along the path.

131. Sir Henry passed their position and then struck out along the path, upwards behind them. The three men peered into the darkness after him and as they did so they were first alerted by the sound and the then the vision of the utmost horror. It was the hound, so long spoken of, now a truly fearsome reality.

132. Holmes and Watson each fired one shot at the beast, one or both of which met their target but still the beast bounded on after Sir Henry and in a moment he was taken by the throat and brought to the ground. Holmes and Watson sped across the ground between them and another five rounds were fired into the flanks of the beast, and at last it fell.

133. I have seen the carcass with my own eyes and never have I seen a hound of such a size. It was a most fearsome sight even in death, a massive bloodhound and mastiff cross. Holmes and Watson must be celebrated for their fortitude in tackling such a demon.

134. Sir Henry was shaken but thankfully, otherwise uninjured. On returning to Merripits House in search of Stapleton there was no trace of him, however, in an upstairs room they discovered his wife, bound and badly beaten, lashed to a beam in the centre of the room. It was she who directed them the following day to the hidden lair in the very depths of Grimpen Mire. Having discovered his pathway they found beside it Sir Henry's missing boot, taken from him in London and evidently used to provide the hound his scent, now cast aside in his flight.

135. Then and now we can find no trace of Stapleton. We have explored every yard of pathway on and around Grimpen Mire and we are certain that he did not pass beyond it. Those same officers who searched for Selden were despatched to cover familiar ground but can find no trace of Stapleton. It would appear that he is lost to the mire, probably at or near the spot where the boot was discovered.

136. We have examined his lair and found a pit containing sheep bones, no doubt feed for the hound. Also found were preparations containing phosphor paste which Mr Holmes believes was applied to the beast's mouth to affect a glow and to make the hound appear a greater abomination to any who saw it, not that such great theatre was ever required.

137. I am advised by Doctor Mortimer that while Sir Henry is making a good recovery from his experience, he is still too feeble to be interviewed by police regarding events and that a voyage at sea has been prescribed to restore his wits and vigour. It is my intention upon his return to interview both he and Doctor Mortimer regarding their failure to report the whereabouts of Selden.

138. In the immediate aftermath, Detective Inspector Lestrade did extend me the courtesy of coming to see me and will be submitting a report to his superiors, a copy of which will be furnished to me, and will in time be attached to these papers as will a statement each from Mr Holmes and Doctor Watson.

139. In conclusion, as detailed at Para. 135, there is every indication, but no evidence, that Stapleton, or more accurately Mr Baskerville, was lost to the mire at a point along the pathway which led to where the hound was tethered. We have dredged as far as we dare venture into Grimpen Mire but that ground has no history of giving up its dead.

140. Sir, the evidence in this case speaks for itself. Mr Baskerville of Merripits House had designs upon the estates of Baskerville Hall and so set about a liaison with Miss Lyons in order to contrive a circumstance that would induce the ailing, but wary Sir Charles to meet at the picket gate in order that he might unleash the hound upon him. Driven by fear from the apparition at the gate, Sir Charles, as planned, fell dead.

141. Possibly he may have imagined that the way was then clear to step out from his guise as Stapleton and in some fashion claim the estate. What he could not have foreseen was the tenacity of Doctor Mortimer in tracking down Sir Henry and so had to develop a plan to do away with him also.

142. He then set about following Doctor Mortimer to London and having tracked him down, either stole or arranged the theft of Sir Henry's boots from outside his suite at the Northumberland Hotel in order to provide his hound with a scent. His plan may have started to unravel at the very moment of its inception when Mrs Baskerville attempted to warn off Sir Henry from travelling to Devonshire by means of her letter cut from the Times.

143. Having failed in that regard, there is clear empathy when she first meets Sir Henry which her scheming husband puts to good use. The unexpected attraction for Baskerville's wife demonstrated by Sir Henry and the frequent visits to Merripits House, provided Baskerville with the ideal opportunity to have the hound kill his victim.

144. In terms of Mr Baskerville's presumed demise on Grimpen Mire, I have already expressed the view that had he lived and been detained, he would have felt the rope about his neck for the murder of Sir Charles and the attempted murder of Sir Henry as surely as if he had fired a pistol at their heads. His foul instrument was simply doing the master's bidding, of that there is absolutely no doubt.

145.	I would have difficulty I must confess, in persuading the presiding magistrate of a case in relation to the death of the convict Selden. Unless Mr Holmes and Doctor Watson can provide evidence of this being anything other than a tragic accident, there the matter would have to rest as I believe there was neither actual sighting of the hound in the vicinity nor any evidence of a deliberate release of it by Mr Baskerville.

146.	We can surmise that Selden was mistaken for Sir Henry as he was wearing some of his old clothes, however, there is no evidence to support this theory.

147.	Fortunately, the Good Lord has been watchful over these parishes and has spared the lives of many good souls and taken those who side with the devil.

148.    I believe Mr Holmes and Doctor Watson should consider themselves extremely fortunate that their guesswork and taste for adventure has not cost them their lives. Mr Holmes in particular was most certainly reckless in the extreme by hiding on the moor. Selden or the hound could have taken him at any time and there would not have been a shred of evidence. Of equal concern was the fact that scores of armed police officers and prison guards were scouring the moor and could have mistaken him for the felon.

149.    As regards the involvement of Detective Inspector Lestrade. I have made my views clear to the individual officer and will do so to his superiors. I will not countenance officers from other forces arriving unannounced and meddling in the affairs of the Devon County Constabulary.

150. Might I respectfully ask that a formal record of our concern is sent to the Metropolitan Police.

Submitted

R. P. Johns
Detective Superintendent
Devon County Constabulary

V. R

Her Majesty's Coroners Office

Mortuary — *Tavistock*     Date of Examination — *17ᵗʰ October 1889*

Deceased — *Selden Arthur*     Date of Birth — *14ᵗʰ August 1851*

Place of Death — *Black Tor, Dartmoor*     Date of Death — *16ᵗʰ October 1889*

Examined By — *Prof. J. Kennedy*     Released for Burial — *17ᵗʰ October 1889*

Physical Examination –

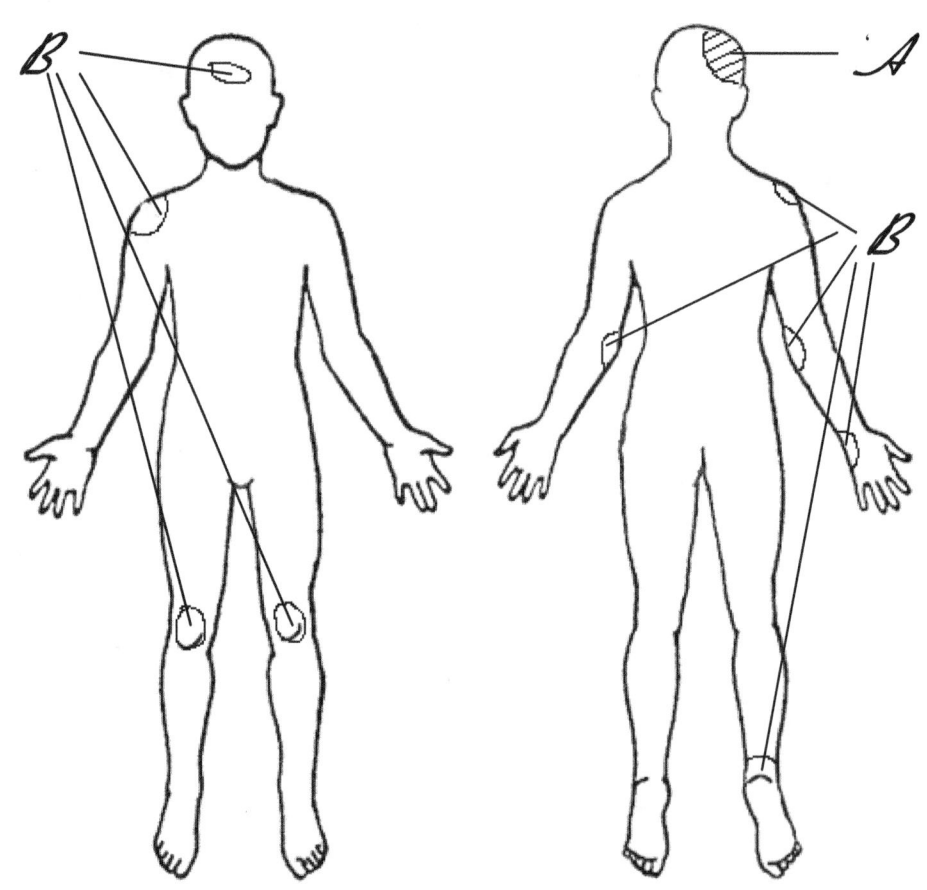

Post Mortem Examination –

I conducted my examination at Tavistock Mortuary commencing at 4.50pm.

The corpse was identified to me by Sergeant Allen of HMP Dartmoor as being that of Arthur Selden, a convict.

I was assisted by a Mr Lee, Principal Mortuary Assistant who prepared the abdominal cavity for inspection.

Due to the evident nature of the trauma I conducted an examination of the Cervical Vertebrae and detected a fracture of C2 and C3. The spinal cord was completely severed.

I also explored the site of a depressed cranial fracture to the right side. This site is marked at A on the diagram. The depression measured 4 inches across and the depression sank to a depth of 1 inch at the centre. The hair around the site was flecked with varieties of lichen and moss. There was little sign of brain haemorrhage despite considerable damage to the tissue.

There were several sites of bruising at various extremities; these are marked at B on the diagram.

Post Mortem Examination –

I conducted a cursory examination of the vital organs and noted the presence of mild sclerosis of the liver and moderate congestion of the pulmonary artery.

No disease or degeneration was present in other organs but there was evidence of malnourishment, poor dental hygiene and sheep tick infestation about the ankles.

Determination –

I am given to understand that this man was about the moor when he fell into a gully strewn with rocks and other material. Immediately following his fall he was attended to by a qualified medical professional who determined that life was extinct.

I conclude that death was caused by a fracture of the cervical vertebrae C2 and C3 consistent with a fall in rough terrain. The cranial fracture was in itself a fatal injury as there would have been fatal haemorrhaging from the site, however, in this instance it proved incidental as death would have been instantaneous from spinal shock. The other marks about the body are consistent with a fall.

Professor James Kennedy

# Metropolitan Police

## Criminal Records Office

Name - *Selden Arthur George*  CRO No. - *14184/81 G*

| Date | Court | Offence | Sentence | Spent |
|------|-------|---------|----------|-------|
| 4.9.1881 | Marylebone Mags Court | Juvenile Larceny S.1 Larceny Act 1867 | 6 months impt. | |
| 18.8.1882 | Marylebone Mags Court | Sale of poor Horseflesh S.8 Sale of Food Act 1864 | 3 mths impt | |
| 13.4.84 | Harrow Mags Ct | 1) Burglary Dwelling S.4 Larceny Act 1867 2) Burglary Dwelling S.4 Larceny Act 1867 | 2yrs impt. 3yrs impt. Consec. | |
| 28.8.1888 | Central Criminal Court | 1) Murder 2) Murder | Death by Hanging | |
| | | *This sentence of Death by Hanging was commuted to Detention at Her Majesty's Pleasure* | | |

Chapter Two

# The Police Witness Statements

This statement (consisting of: *7* pages each signed by me) is true to the best of my knowledge and belief and I make it knowing that, if it is tendered in evidence, I shall be liable to prosecution if I have wilfully stated anything which I know to be false or do not believe to be true.

Statement Of - *John Barrymore*     Taken down by - *PC 455 Bell DCC*

Date - *6ᵗʰ May 1889*

My name is John Barrymore and together with my wife Eliza were employed in service in the employ of the late Sir Charles Baskerville at Baskerville Hall.

We have been in service at the Hall these last two years since the return of Sir Charles from overseas.

My duties were to attend to Sir Charles as his manservant, preparing clothes and boots for riding and so on; in addition I would serve at table.

I can think of no finer gentleman than Sir Charles, he was a most thoughtful employer and generous to a fault as many in these parts will bear witness.

Signed - *J Barrymore*     Date - *6ᵗʰ May 1889*

In recent months I was aware that Sir Charles was becoming more on edge, nothing was imparted to me and so I am none the wiser as to the cause. I was though, asked to call on Dr Mortimer to attend Sir Charles quite frequently these last few spring months.

On more than one occasion of late I would to respond to Sir Charles only to find him seated in his study or rooms, in some discomfort, short of breath at times and his complexion an unhealthy pale. On such occasions I would loosen his collar and cravat and dispatch Perkins, the groom, to summon Dr Mortimer at Meldon House without delay.

On the morning of Saturday 4th May, Sir Charles announced to us his intention to depart the following day by train to London for a period. After serving at breakfast and laying out Sir Charles' tweeds for dressing, I rode to Buckfastleigh Railway Station to purchase a travel ticket against Sir Charles' account.

I returned to Baskerville Hall at noon to help my wife prepare Sir Charles' things for his travels

Signed - J Barrymore                    Date - 6th May 1889

That evening I served at table for Sir Charles who dined alone at 8pm. His dinner consisted of a single course of fresh duck and vegetables, all estate fare, prepared as usual by my sister. Sir Charles was a light eater and drank red wine in moderation and would partake of a glass of port after a meal of red meats only.

Having attended to Sir Charles at table my wife and I were told that would be all for the evening save to respond to the bell if required.

As was customary, Sir Charles would venture out from the Hall from the main door for a walk sometime around 10pm. This walk would vary in duration, but never in route as, for some reason, Sir Charles would never venture far from the Hall whether by day or by night.

After our own supper, which was always taken in the kitchen and prior to retiring each evening, our final duties were to douse candles and dampen fires. I would make a final walk through the Hall to ensure all was well and to secure the front door after Sir Charles had returned from his walk. I would generally retire at midnight and rise at 6am.

Signed - *J Barrymore*                                    Date - *6th May 1889*

100

That Saturday evening I performed my duties as usual, and shortly before midnight I went to lock the main door but found it still ajar. I quickly called at Sir Charles door and on receiving no reply went in to find no trace of him.

I lit an oil lantern and took an oilskin and went outside to find Sir Charles. The night was cold and the air was damp from a day of rain. I ventured round the Hall, calling all the while but could find no trace until I reached the Yew Avenue, as we call it, a pathway of some 150 yards that extends from the Hall to the moor.

Some 100 yards along the gravel path I saw Sir Charles, fallen to his face. I rushed to his assistance but could not rouse any response; indeed, just from taking his wrist I could feel his flesh a deathly cold. I knew Sir Charles had passed away at that spot.

His feet were nearest the house and his hands were both clenched about the gravel beneath him. I could see no sign of injury about his body, or any sign of disturbance around him but still I feared the worst.

Signed – J Barrymore                    Date - 6th May 1889

I ran to the stables and roused Perkins to ride to Dr Mortimer's and to his credit he was up and gone in no time.

From the stables I returned round the far side of the house to the front door where I took another jacket against the cold. I also called upon my wife but did not fully say what my thoughts were save to say Sir Charles had taken a fall and I returned immediately to the yew avenue to wait with Sir Charles for Dr Mortimer.

I could hear the house clock strike the first hour just before the Doctor's carriage arrived. When I heard the sound of his carriage I ran to the front of the Hall to meet Dr Mortimer and I led him to where Sir Charles lay.

I cannot have been a pleasant task for the Doctor as I knew him to be e good friend of Sir Charles as well as his doctor. I held my lamp for the Doctor to see as he went about examining the body. He held a glass to his mouth and then turned Sir Charles onto his back.

Signed - J Barrymore                    Date - 6th May 1889

102

I recoiled at the sight and was barely able to save the lantern from falling from my hand. Sir Charles' face was cut with gravel but his features were twisted and disfigured in some horror. Had I not seen it for myself I would not believe such a tale from anyone, and I pray each nigh that I should not have to die in such a fashion.

Doctor Mortimer steadied himself and after pressing the glass to the mouth once more he checked his pocket-watch then told me that Sir Charles was dead.

Doctor Mortimer busied himself about the scene, venturing along the path and back to the picket gate. The decision was made to send Perkins for a Constable while Doctor Mortimer and I carried the body of Sir Charles into the boot room. A sheet was placed over the body.

I left Doctor Mortimer to explain the tragedy to my wife. After some while, I cannot remember the hour, a Police Sergeant arrived by horse and spent time in questioning my sister and I, and Doctor Mortimer. My wife became more distressed and was seen in private briefly by the Doctor. Myself, I slept only briefly after the police and Doctor left us, Sir Charles rested where he was laid until morning.

Signed - J Barrymore                    Date - 6th May 1889

I rose at 7am and shortly after 8am was alerted by the return of Doctor Mortimer. I was much relieved as no explanation had been provided to me as what to do with the body of Sir Charles. Shortly after, two constables arrived in the Coroner's wagon and removed the body of Sir Charles, I am told, to Tavistock.

My wife and I have touched nothing of Sir Charles' things and his rooms have been locked from that day to this. We have been given leave to remain at Baskerville Hall on the instruction of Doctor Mortimer to whom we are beholden.

J Barrymore

Witness Statement

This statement (consisting of: *2* pages each signed by me) is true to the best of my knowledge and belief and I make it knowing that, if it is tendered in evidence, I shall be liable to prosecution if I have wilfully stated anything which I know to be false or do not believe to be true.

Statement Of - *Joshua Perkins*          Taken down by - *PC 455 Bell DCC*

Date - *6ᵗʰ May 1889*

My name is Joshua Perkins. I am employed as groom at Baskerville Hall. I have been in service at the Hall for two years.

My duties were to attend to the care of four horses, two geldings, two mares and I have a room in the stable block. When told by Mr Barrymore I would saddle the fittest mount for Sir Charles or ready them for his carriage if asked. I would see to the horses upon their return.

Sir Charles did not ride these last months, nor did I see much of him in person, save glimpses of him around the Hall or walking as he did most evenings. I have been asked if I saw anything of Sir Charles last Saturday and I did not, until nightfall.

Signed - *P*                              Date - *6ᵗʰ May 1889*

I called at the kitchen door as usual to collect my tray of supper and I saw Mr and Mrs Barrymore about to eat at the kitchen table.

Well after dark I was roused from sleep by Mr Barrymore who was in a very agitated state. He told me to waste no time in riding to the Doctor's house in Grimpen. I have ridden this journey several times of late having been asked to get the Doctor for Sir Charles on many occasions. The Doctor was awake when I called and I relayed the message as told. I then returned to Baskerville Hall and returned to my room.

I was called from my room some time later and told by Mr Barrymore to fetch a Constable from Buckfastleigh. As I rode a fresh mare from the stable I saw the Doctor's carriage outside Baskerville Hall.

It was still dark when I arrived at Buckfastleigh Police Station where I relayed my instructions to the officer on duty. He instructed me to return to Baskerville Hall directly, which I did.

I have been told that Sir Charles died that night. I did not see or hear anything out of the ordinary. ∫ Mark made by J Perkins

Signed - ∫                                Date - 6th May 1889

106

*This statement (consisting of:* **4** *pages each signed by me) is true to the best of my knowledge and belief and I make it knowing that, if it is tendered in evidence, I shall be liable to prosecution if I have wilfully stated anything which I know to be false or do not believe to be true.*

Statement Of - *Eliza Barrymore*       Taken down by - *PC 455 Bell DCC*

Date - *6ᵗʰ May 1889*

My name is Eliza Barrymore and I have been married to my husband John these last eighteen years. I am employed in service as cook and domestic help for Sir Charles Baskerville at Baskerville Hall. We have been in service at the Hall for over two years.

My duties were to attend to laundry and cooking for Sir Charles and his occasional guests including Mr Stapleton and Doctor Mortimer, by far the most frequent caller at the Hall, due in most part to the fact that Sir Charles was suffering these months with an ailment of the heart, I believe.

On Saturday 4ᵗʰ May, Sir Charles announced at breakfast that he was to leave for London the very next day. I was somewhat vexed at the notion as I had only just replenished the larder with several sides of fresh meat and had fruit and wine on order.

Signed - E Barrymore                    Date - *6ᵗʰ May 1889*

My husband rode out in the morning to obtain tickets for the rail journey and as Sir Charles busied himself with his papers, I began to organize his effects for the journey. On my husbands return, most of Sir Charles' clothing was ready to be packed in his trunks and all that remained was for my husband to prepare shoes and boots for town.

I served Sir Charles a light luncheon of ham sandwiches and savoury preserve with tea. I served the meal upon a tray in the study. Within the hour I was summonsed by bell whereupon I collected the tray and left Sir Charles seated in his wing chair which had been moved into the window. I presumed from that, that Sir Charles would be reading or writing in his journal.

I last saw Sir Charles at 8pm when I assisted my husband in serving dinner to table. I noted that Sir Charles had changed from his daywear into a suit of tweed, his usual evening attire. Shortly after Sir Charles meal had been cleared, Perkins, the groom, called at the kitchen door for his tray, after which my husband and I sat for our own supper.

Signed - E Barrymore                    Date - 6th May 1889

After doing the dishes, I returned to the dining room and doused the candles and knocked down the fire to a low smoulder. Sir Charles had retired to the study where a small fire had been set for him. I left my husband reading and went to bed at 11pm, ready to rise at 6am. My husband would usually retire around midnight having doused what candles were lit and locked the door after Sir Charles late walk.

Sometime after midnight I became aware of a great commotion and activity at the stables. I heard a single horse ride off. I put on a heavy gown and went downstairs to find my husband in the hallway. He told me that Sir Charles had taken a fall on the gravel path by the yew avenue, I was not to be concerned but as a precaution, Perkins had been sent for Doctor Mortimer.

My husband dressed himself in a woollen coat and oilskin and returned outside to be with Sir Charles, I was to keep watch for the arrival of the Doctor.

It was near 1am when the Doctor's carriage arrived. He was met at the door by my husband before they both set off in the direction of the Yew Avenue.

Signed - E Barrymore                    Date - 6th May 1889

After some ten minutes or so, I heard a single horse ride off from the Hall, following which my husband and the doctor returned to the house from the kitchen door, it was then that I was told that Sir Charles had suffered heart failure and was dead.

I felt unwell and had to be seated. The doctor and my husband told me that the body was to be brought into the house pending the arrival of the police. A short time later they arrived back at the door, between the carrying the body of Sir Charles. I could not bear to look upon the poor soul and retired to the dining room.

The doctor attended to me and provided a medication to calm my nerves but I was only able to manage a few hours of fitful sleep until the morning when more police arrived and removed the body.

E. Barrymore

Signed - E. Barrymore                    Date - 6th May 1889

110

Witness Statement

This statement (consisting of: *5* pages each signed by me) is true to the best of my knowledge and belief and I make it knowing that, if it is tendered in evidence, I shall be liable to prosecution if I have wilfully stated anything which I know to be false or do not believe to be true.

Statement Of - *Dr James Mortimer*     Taken down by -

Date -     *7ᵗʰ May 1889*

I qualified in medicine at the Royal College of Surgeons London in 1849 and have been practicing as a Medical Practitioner these last 40 years.

In 1884 I retired as House Surgeon at the Charing Cross Hospital in London to light practice and took up the position as Medical Officer for the parishes of Grimpen Thorsley and High Barrow. I reside at Meldon House, Grimpen.

In April 1887 I became acquainted with Sir Charles Baskerville on his taking up residence in Baskerville Hall. I came to know him as both patient and friend. In recent months Sir Charles had been showing signs of affliction and asked me to attend him on several occasions. My examinations indicated that Sir Charles was suffering from mild congestion of the heart for which I recommended gentle daily exercise and red wine with meals. Symptoms such as mild breathlessness palpitations and loss of sensation to the extremities would manifest themselves after vigorous exertions.

Signed -   *J Mortimer*     Date - *7ᵗʰ May 1889*

Sir Charles was a private gentleman, extremely munificent as all in these parishes will attest, he was generally possessed of a quiet, thoughtful disposition, but of late, I confess I found him somewhat troubled in thought. He became restive and uneasy in his situation at Baskerville Hall.

Not wishing this agitation to impinge on his already delicate constitution I advised Sir Charles to take a sojourn in London in the hope that the distractions of the capital would allow him time to recover his vigour. I was supported in this view by Mr Stapleton, a near neighbour who visited Sir Charles on several occasions. Regrettably, Sir Charles was due to depart Baskerville Hall for his residence in Brompton yesterday, Monday 6th May, only two days after his death.

I last saw Sir Charles alive in the afternoon of Wednesday 1st May. I found him to be in his usual state of health.

At approximately 00.40 hrs I was engrossed in study when I was disturbed by a caller to the house. The man was Joshua Perkins a man known to me as a patient and groom at Baskerville Hall. He was in an agitated state and the condition of his mount suggested that he had been ridden hard to Grimpen. Perkins stated that an accident had befallen Sir Charles and that Barrymore sought my attendance as a matter of some urgency.

Signed - *J Mortimer*                                      Date - 7th May 1889

112

Without attending to his mount, Perkins rode off. I immediately prepared my carriage and made directly for Baskerville Hall, arriving just after 1am. From the house, Barrymore led me some length along a gravel path bounded by yew trees. At a point some 10yds from the house, in the glow from Barrymore's lamp I saw the form of Sir Charles.

He was dressed in his usual evening wardrobe of tweed jacket and breeches and tan boots. He was lying face down on the gravel path, feet nearest the house, head towards the moor, in the middle of the path. His hands were clenched tight about some gravel.

The night was damp and chill and I removed a small looking glass from my medical bag and placed it at the mouth of Sir Charles. No sign of breath was evident upon the glass. I checked for a pulse, first upon the neck and then at the left wrist. There was no pulse and the flesh was cold although rigor-mortis was not present.

In the light of Barrymore's lamp I rolled Sir Charles onto his back and was immediately taken aback by the contortions upon his face, the like of which I have never seen before in all my years of medicine. The eyes were fixed wide open, the pupils were dilated. His brow was furrowed and the mouth was agape as if in exclamation. The skin about the face had been cut raw by the gravel, so too the palms of the hands.

Signed - *J. Mortimer*                                          Date - 7th May 1889

113

The body bore no sign of mortal injury and the clothing was unmarked and intact save for marks upon the knees of the breeches and scrapes to the toes of the boots, consistent with a fall. I listened for breath and once more placed my glass at the mouth, there were no signs of breath, no signs of life and so, at 1.05am I pronounced life extinct.

When I examined the scene in proximity to the body I could distinguish one set of footmarks upon the gravel path leading to the point where Sir Charles lay. Barrymore and I had approached on a separate line. I noted that the few yards of footmarks immediately behind the body from a point at the moor gate were different in definition to those leading from the house. At the moor gate I found cigar ash in two spots by the gate.

The medical evidence suggests to me that Sir Charles having left the house at 10pm for his usual late evening stroll about the grounds of Baskerville Hall, fell victim to heart failure, the consequences of which were so grave as to leave him contorted and convulsed with pain at the point of death.

I directed that the body be moved into the house and Sir Charles was taken into the boot room where he was laid on the floor and covered with a sheet. I then directed Perkins to ride out to alert the Constable.

Signed - J Mortimer                                    Date - 7th May 1889

114

At almost 03.45hrs a Police Sergeant Brigg arrived and I identified the body of Sir Charles to him. I was questioned by the officer as to events within my knowledge following which, due both to the lateness of the hour and the inclement weather; it was decided to leave the body in the house until the daylight hours.

Following the departure of Sergeant Briggs I attended briefly to Mrs Barrymore who had become understandably distressed by the tragic events. At just after 05.00hrs I left Baskerville Hall and returned to Meldon House

*J Mortimer*

Signed - *J Mortimer*                                     Date - 7th May 1889

This statement (consisting of: **8** pages each signed by me) is true to the best of my knowledge and belief and I make it knowing that, if it is tendered in evidence, I shall be liable to prosecution if I have wilfully stated anything which I know to be false or do not believe to be true.

Statement Of - *John Barrymore*          Taken down by - *DS Williams*

Date -          *21ˢᵗ October 1889*

My name is John Barrymore and together with my wife Eliza, I am employed in service to Sir Henry Baskerville at Baskerville Hall.

On Wednesday 1ˢᵗ October 1889 my wife and I were alone in the house as had been the case since the death of Sir Charles in May of this year. On the instructions of Doctor Mortimer we were preparing the house for the arrival of the new master, Sir Henry Baskerville, whom it was anticipated would shortly take up residence.

At around 8pm I was alerted to a noise at the kitchen door, the sound of something small being thrown against it. The only person with cause to call at that door with any regularity is Joshua Perkins, the estate groom who lives in the stable block.

Signed - *J Barrymore*          Date *21ˢᵗ October 1889*

He calls at the door for his supper tray each evening with a sturdy rap at the glass pane so this was not he.

The weather that evening was foul; a heavy western squall was being driven across the moor by high winds. I took a storm lantern and opened the kitchen door and the force of the wind blew the door full open. I could neither hear nor see anything in the force of the rain and simply called out yonder.

A man sprang at me from the darkness, taking me from the side. He said to me Take a care not to move too swift, mind or Ill slit your throat. Fearing for my life I let this fellow edge me back into the kitchen where he released me before shutting the door.

As he did so he darted to our kitchen basin and from it grabbed our sharpest knife. He plainly had no knife when he captured me but he was fully armed now.

He edged around the kitchen and took our bread loaf and began taking mouthfuls of it, he then drank my ale. All the time he used one hand to eat and held the knife towards me with the other.

Signed - J Barrymore                    Date - 21st October 1889

This man was wearing dark clothes, almost rags and he was soaked through to his filthy skin. His dark hair was lank and filthy and I really did not know what to think of him other than he was some crazed loner from off the moor. I just stood watching him gorge on whatever food he found in view.

At that moment my wife Eliza came into the kitchen and dashed to my side when she saw the intruder. I made her stand behind me. I told the man to take what food he wanted, to take an oilskin but cause us no harm.

He said "Would you think I come here to cause my dearest Elizabeth any harm".

I felt my wife edge out from behind me. She then shouted out "Arthur, my sweet Jesus is that you" before running directly at the man. I lunged forward and caught just enough of her apron to hold her but she spun and said to me "John leave me, its my brother, its Arthur"

My heart rose with relieve that this was not some lunatic then sank with the knowledge that if this was her brother all right, then he was none other than Arthur Selden the savage Notting Hill murderer.

Signed - J Barrymore                                        Date - 21st October 1889

My wife talked little of her brother, she heard enough from me to know what I thought of him and the matter was seldom, if ever raised again.

My wife was in hysterics, one moment berating this man, the next embracing him.

Selden looked directly at me and said "I'm here to see my sister, not to cause you harm. I'm escaped from Princetown and they'll be here after me in quick time. Hide me and feed me for a few days and I'm out of your hair. I've passage planned from Plymouth a week from now to the South Americas."

With that he put down the knife and Eliza grabbed it and threw it in the sink.

She motioned me from the kitchen and we left Selden and went to our parlour. My wife was sobbing into her apron and I embraced her. I agreed for her sake to shield this man for a week, no more.


The guards and the hounds were on the estate for that night. One guard came to call at the hall to bid us beware but did not ask to search about the place.

Signed - *J Barrymore*                    Date - *21st October 1889*

119

Selden bathed and slept that night in a loft room. I burnt his rags the following day with some leaves and branches gathered from the courtyard.

On 2nd October I was in the loft with Selden going through some old clothes when there was a call to our door from the telegram boy. I could hear him talking to my wife and all the time I motioned to Selden to keep silent. My wife came to the bottom of the stair and read the wire from Doctor Mortimer and I said something or other to my wife to write in reply but cannot recall the word. I was in fear Selden might move to pounce for the boy.

As the boy left I went to the kitchen and read the telegram and at that moment Selden appeared from the loft. I made to read the wire again with Selden at my very side. I knew from that he could not read and so I told him a falsehood - that Sir Henry was on way from London and he would have to be away from the house without delay.

Signed - J Barrymore                    Date - 21st October 1889

My ploy worked and the following morning Selden left Baskerville Hall to retreat to the moor. Our arrangement was that when food was available I would signal to the moor from empty upstairs windows with a candle moved in the sign of the cross. My signal would meet with a light from the moor to where I should take the provisions. Should the signal not meet these arrangements then Selden was to presume our plan was compromised.

On Saturday 4th October I was at Baskerville Hall for the arrival of Sir Henry and another gentleman called Doctor Watson and having set to unpacking the gentlemens things and serving at table my wife and I retired to bed. I was woken several times through the night by my wife who became more and more distressed as the night wore on at the thought of her brother out alone on the moor and what would become of him should they capture him. I did my best to console her but she cried for moist of the night.

On Sunday 5th October and for every second night thereafter I would wait for the house to hush in the early hours and then make my way to the second floor and give my signal to Selden beyond on the moor.

Signed - J Barrymore                    Date - 21st October 1889

I would wait for his response and set my mind to where his light might be, and then head off with food and laundry. I even took him some of Sir Henrys clothes that he had gifted to me, but were too small.

On Wednesday 15th October, in the small hours I was about to make my signal at the window when I was discovered by Sir Henry and Doctor Watson. My signal was not complete though Doctor Watson motioned the candle about the window in such a fashion as Selden would know to be on his guard.

While I was being questioned by Sir Henry, my wife Eliza came into the room on hearing the commotion told everything about her brother. I now know that Sir Henry and Doctor Watson gave chase that night but failed to capture him.

Later that same day I told Sir Henry and Doctor Mortimer of a find that my wife had made in the grate of the fire in what was Sir Charles study in the weeks after his death. I cannot recall the exact date but it was the lower portion of a letter in an envelope postmarked Coombe Tracey.

Signed - J Barrymore                    Date - 21st October 1889

The fragment read - Please, please, as you are a gentleman, burn this letter, and be at the gate by ten 'o clock." Beneath it were signed the initials L. L. As it was his last, I recall that letter arriving in the post for Sir Charles on 4th May, the day he died.

I asked the gentleman to allow Selden to escape these shores in exchange, to which they agreed. I also mentioned that Selden had told me of an agent about the more, not police or guards, possibly a bounty hunter who was in some lair lying low.

On 1st October I received news that Selden had met his death in a fall on the moor escaping his pursuers, the police said. The next day I rode to Princetown Prison where I identified the body of Arthur Selden.

I say now that neither my wife nor I had any knowledge of or any hand in, his escape. He may have been my wifes brother but he was nothing to me

. J Barrymore

Signed - J Barrymore                    Date 21st October 1889

Chapter Three

# Other Correspondence

Doctor James Mortimer
Meldon House
Grimpen
Devonshire
England

10<sup>th</sup> June 1889

Dear Sirs

I act on behalf of the estate of the late Sir Charles Baskerville who met his demise on 5<sup>th</sup> May this year, without issue.

He leaves an estate consisting of land, property, livestock and holdings of a considerable value which now pass to the next of kin, in this case, Sir Henry Baskerville (Born 14.02.1857).

My initial enquiries suggest that Sir Henry has land in the state of Vermont, however, my information is limited and I am unable to assist you further in that regard.

My instructions are this, that you make enquiries of an urgent nature to locate and establish contact with Sir Henry and to make him aware of his situation here in Devonshire. If you could telegram the details as you have them. I propose to make payment of $20.00 on account for your services. I trust this meets with your approval.

Yours Faithfully

James Mortimer DR

125

Pinkerton's National Detective Agency

Madison, New York City, New York U.S.A.

14th July 1889

Dear Dr Mortimer,

In confirmation of our telegraph wire of 10th July, we have
succeeded in tracing Mr Henry Baskerville to properties at Adaire,
Fredericton, State of New Brunswick, Canada.

Our representative has called upon Mr Baskerville and presented
your credentials as requested. Mr Baskerville will be writing to
you as a matter of some urgency and may we suggest that you confirm
in writing your intentions with him at your earliest convenience.

Our final invoice in the sum of $49.50 is attached for your
attention.


Assuring you of our best attention at all times
Your servant


P Kelly

Pinkertons

Doctor James Mortimer
Meldon House
Grimpen,
Devonshire,
England

18th July 1889

Dear Sir Henry

Please allow me to introduce myself. I act on behalf of the estate of the late Sir Charles Baskerville who met an unexpected and early death on 5th May this year.

Sir Charles died without issue and our enquiries give us every reason to believe that you are the sole heir to his estate. As the executor of his estate, I can advise you that there is a considerable fortune involved: however, I feel it would be inappropriate to discuss such delicate matters further by means of a postal letter.

In terms of lands and property, the estate consists of tenanted agricultural land, tenanted property, livestock and holdings of a considerable value in addition to the magnificent family home, Baskerville Hall which has undergone a comprehensive programme of considerable modernisation in these last two years at the hand of Sir Charles.

Sir Charles was well-beloved in these parishes renowned as a man of great benevolence who was greatly admired and is widely mourned still.

I would be most grateful if you could give some indication regarding your intentions towards the Baskerville estate in order that I might advise Messrs. Hall Cartwright & Co. Solicitors who assist me in this matter.

Yours Faithfully

James Mortimer DR

Henry Baskerville
Adaire
Fredericton
New Brunswick
Canada

30th July 1889


My Dear Dr Mortimer

I was most surprised to receive the attention of Pilkington's men these last few weeks and also delighted to receive you letter of the 14th inst.

I remember little of Baskerville Hall, childhood conversations and the like, but very much look forward to meeting with you and visiting the Hall at the earliest opportunity.

I have instructed my attorney to make direct contact with Messrs Hall, Cartwright & Co and in the meantime I will make arrangements for a passage to Southampton as soon as my commitments here allow.

I make no assurances at this stage, save to say I am keenly interested in taking stock of the estate.

Yours,

Henry Baskerville

Chapter Four

# Official Photographs

Fig. 1 -Baskerville Hall

Fig. 2 – The yew avenue at Baskerville Hall

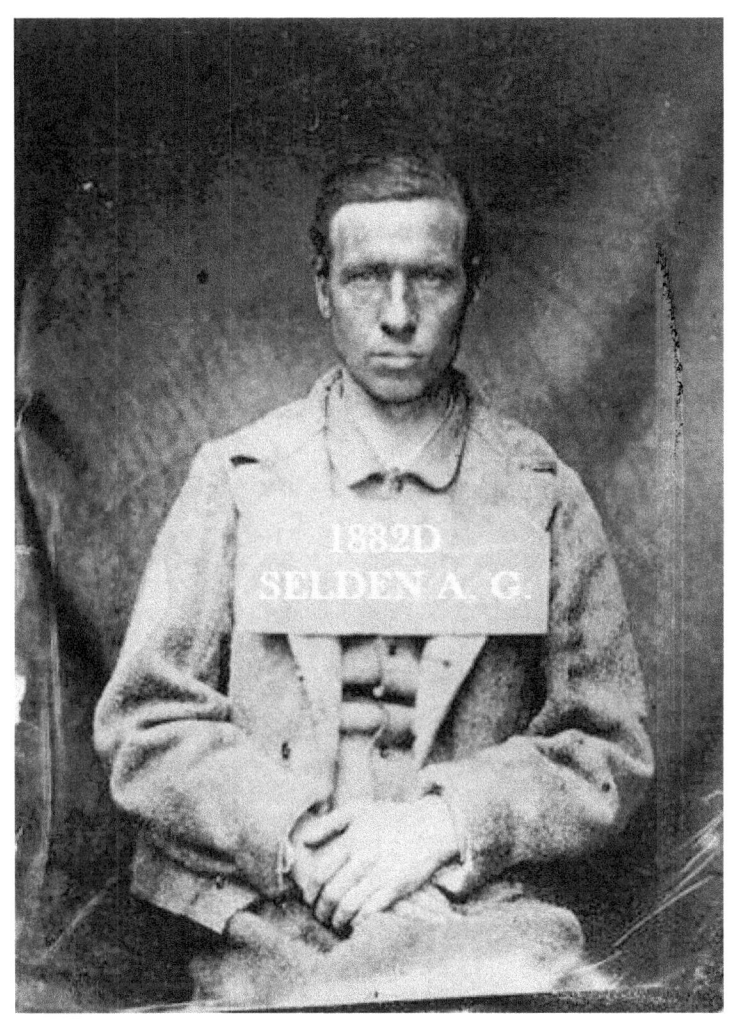

**Fig. 3 – Prison photograph of Albert Selden**

Fig. 4 – The hound where it fell

Chapter Five

# Miscellaneous

# The Western Morning News

Daily News for Devonshire and Cornwall

Monday 19th October 1889

Price - 2d

## HOUND SLAIN

**Last night a wild hound was shot dead near Grimpen Mire following an attack upon the person of Sir Henry Baskerville.**

Reports suggest that Sir Henry was walking home in the company of friends, amongst them the illustrious London sleuth Mr Sherlock Holmes and his associate, Dr J Watson.

The group were attacked by the beast with Sir Henry bravely fending off the first attack suffering personal injury as he did so. Mr Holmes and Dr Watson were both fortunately in possession of revolvers and managed to shoot dead the hound.

In a bizarre twist to the episode, police are searching for the local entomologist Mr Stapleton of nearby Merripit House who is reported missing, feared lost to the mire having been chased by the hound in a similar attack.

More news to follow

## Vessel Lost

Volunteers were this morning searching the coastline to the north of Black Rock at Widemouth Bay for survivors or wreckage from the vessel Brea from Bude. The vessel was seen in some difficulty just after sunset in difficult waters and has not returned to port.

The Brea is owned and operated by PKF Shipping in nearby Holsworthy

## FELON DEAD

The Governor of HMP Dartmoor has confirmed that as we reported yesterday, the escaped felon Arthur Selden died as a result of a fall in which he broke his neck.

At the time of his death Selden was being tracked down by Mr Sherlock Holmes and Dr Watson who had been called in to assist the prison authorities

His burial will take place within the walls of the prison.

## Prized Bull Sold Overseas

The award winning prize bull from the Cranworthy Estate farm has been sold to an Irish cattle breeder.

The bull will shortly travel by sea to Rosslaire and onwards to a new home in Athlone, Co. Mullingar where breeder Dr O'Keefe believes the bull will improve the herd at the Adaire Estate Farm.

## New Rail Line

Great Western Railway are set to announce that a new railway line is to be constructed between Barnstaple and Coomb Martin. Work will commence in Spring next year and the spur will take 2 years to complete.

Weather -

Fair, light winds 48F

# Chapter Six

# Explanatory Notes

# Explanatory Notes

**The Death of Sir Charles Baskerville –**

Doctor Mortimer has clearly identified in Sir Charles the signs and symptoms of progressive coronary heart disease. Without recourse to modern surgical intervention, terminal decline was almost inevitable and the remedy at the time was simply for rest and dietary adjustments.

Sir Charles' condition was, as we know, compounded by the stress of his strong belief in the legend of the Hound of the Baskervilles, a fear confided to Dr Mortimer and the principal reason behind the planned sojourn to London, away from Baskerville Hall.

It appears that the good Doctor was rather indiscreet and broadcast the gravity of Sir Charles' condition too freely; reaching as it did the eager ears of Stapleton, As a consequence, the engineered confrontation with the Hound at the picket gate that fateful night was enough to kill Sir Charles outright.

When Barrymore discovered the body of his master on the gravel path he was well advised to send for Doctor Mortimer as he was not to know if Sir Charles was merely unconscious or not. It can be argued that the horror etched across Sir Charles' features would have told him all he needed to know, but it certainly wasn't his place to make that assumption.

It cannot have been an easy situation for Doctor Mortimer, having to attend to the death of his good friend in his guise as medical practitioner and at the same time dealing with the realisation, having seen the paw marks left adjacent to the body, that there might after all be some truth in the legend of the Hound.

This obviously plays on his mind to the point where he decides to involve the police but strangely, as soon as Perkins is despatched, Dr Mortimer immediately decides to move the body from the scene and remove it to the boot room. The general rule is – that if they are dead, they are dead, the weather can't hurt them, so leave well alone.

Had there been anything untoward in the death of Sir Charles this would have proved catastrophic to any subsequent enquiry as the variance in indoor and outdoor temperatures would have completely thrown any attempt to determine the time of death, as a human body reduces in core temperature after death by 1°C per hour until it reaches the ambient temperature of its surroundings. Worse still, moving the body would necessarily disturb any forensic or physical evidence on or around it and at the crime scene itself.

Doctor Mortimer's own brief investigation at the gate and at the point where the body lay told him that all was not well yet he makes no mention of these paw marks in his witness statement made just two days later, nor any reference to anything untoward in his submission to the Coroner at the subsequent inquest. Some might also argue that then was the time to engage the services of a consulting detective, not in October when the matter is five months old.

**The attendance of the local Police**

As we can see from the notebook of PS5 Briggs, his attendance at Baskerville Hall is more routine than an investigative masterpiece. His notes conform to the rule and regulation –blank spaces lined-off and initialled, no over-writing, date, time and place recorded – but no more.

He cannot be said to be at all proactive, he makes no examination of the scene other than a cursory glimpse at the spot where Sir Charles fell in fact, he seems to allow himself to be led very much by Doctor Mortimer to the point where he appears too deferential, perhaps somewhat in awe of the circumstances in which he finds himself. Why else go all the way to Baskerville Hall himself in the middle of the night instead of sending one of his Constables unless he thought it so important. Did he allow the status of those concerned in the matter to get the better of his professional judgement?

The practicalities of leaving the body where it lay overnight speak for themselves. For PS 5 Briggs to alert the Coroners officer at that late hour would have been impractical and would have taken several hours in any event.

Much easier to leave the body of Sir Charles in the boot room and have officers from the coroner's office appear with a casket the following morning to remove the remains.

**The Baskerville Post Mortem –**

Where the deceased has been attended to by a qualified practitioner in the two weeks preceding death a post mortem examination is not normally required, and this being the case with Sir Charles who was in regular contact with Doctor Mortimer it is unclear why one was required in this case.

As in all such 'sudden death' cases, the pathologist Professor Kennedy heads for the most likely cause of death – the heart. He would have read the preliminary police notes and completed an examination of the skin noting marks and anything of interest following which Mr Sharp, the mortuary assistant, would have prepared the abdominal cavity for examination by making the primary incision and then rather coarsely cutting away the ribcage and associated visceral tissue.

Even at this preliminary stage, a visual examination of the heart would raise concern as the diseased heart is frequently enlarged. Professor Kennedy would have removed the organ and would have weighed it to confirm what his experienced eye was already telling him. Finally, dissection would have confirmed the extent of the blockage, in this case to the Coronary Artery.

The other vital organs would then be removed in sequence and examined to determine any contributing factors before the cause of death was officially recorded.

**The Inquest**

The inquest at Tavistock Coroners Court on Friday 10<sup>th</sup> May 1889 would have seen Her Majesty's Coroner sitting alone without a jury and no witnesses present. The Devon County Constabulary Coroner's Officer would have opened proceedings by reading from police reports and the statements of the Barrymores, Perkins and Doctor Mortimer before the Coroner himself considered the medical notes and the Post Mortem report.

The inevitable finding of death due to natural causes would have been recorded and proceedings closed with the Coroner's Officer asking permission for the body to be released for burial. A short time later Doctor Mortimer would have seen to the arrangements to register the death and arrange burial.

**Dr Mortimer as trustee –**

Sir Charles died without an heir and it would be common in such circumstances for a prominent friend to be appointed as executor of the estate, particularly so in the case of someone like Sir Charles who was particularly reclusive.

Messrs. Hall, Cartwright & Co. Solicitors would have been glad of the appointment of Doctor Mortimer, particularly so in light of his determination to find an heir rather than have the estate descend into costly administration.

Quite what references the good Doctor makes use of to discover the lineage to Sir Henry in not clear but his persistence and forward thinking in engaging Pinkertons is rewarded when they trace Sir Henry to New Brunswick in Canada.

Sir Henry's sea passage from New York would have seen the S.S. St Louis dock at Cherbourg before continuing to Southampton in just over six days. First class passengers such as Sir Henry would have had onward rail travel to Waterloo arranged for them as part of their passage.

**Engaging Mr Holmes**

The eternal question in all of this, and something that is clearly echoed in the original police reports, is why did Doctor Mortimer approach the esteemed (and so no doubt, costly) Mr Sherlock Holmes in London, rather than approach senior police figures within the Devon County Constabulary.

Certainly his professional standing in the Dartmoor area would have ensured him access to several senior and influential figures, all of whom would surely have been in a position to provide enough manpower to ensure the well-being of such a prominent local figure and potential benefactor as Sir Henry. Indeed, I cannot help but think that by not doing so, by controversially bringing in an 'outsider' in this way, Doctor Mortimer has in fact alienated himself from senior police figures that become dismissive of Holmes and his methods.

Also, why did Doctor Mortimer leave it until the very day that Sir Henry was arriving in London to consult with Holmes. There could have been any number of reasons why Holmes might not be available, he might even decline the case, what then would Doctor Mortimer have done. Quite why he didn't write to Holmes in advance to secure an appointment for his consultation is unclear. The big question in all of this, is what would have happened had Holmes not stepped in to investigate.

We might well have had a new tenant at Baskerville Hall – Mr Stapleton, no less

**Arthur Selden**

One of nature's true unfortunates if ever there was one. A man who evades the noose, and then escape his prison cell but only to have his neck broken taking flight from the Hound.

Selden was the middle of three children born in 1866 into an impoverished family in Harbet Road, Paddington, London, immediately behind where the Paddington Metropole Hotel now stands, and only a stones throw away from the grand houses of Bayswater and Mayfair that would be very much the focus of his criminal activity in later years.

In September 1881 at the tender age of 15 he found himself before Marylebone Magistrates Court charged with Larceny, the theft of a gentleman's pocket watch, for which he was imprisoned for 6 months at Wormwood Scrubs.

On his release in February 1882 he held down a variety of portering jobs at local markets but fell foul of the law again charged with the Sale of poor Horseflesh. His offence was to divert from his portering route delivering fresh horsemeat, swap his load for an equivalent weight of sub-standard flesh from a local farrier, deliver the substituted meat and re-sell the quality meat and pocket the profit. He was sentenced to three months imprisonment.

A few years on the straight and narrow saw him back in the arms of the law once more in April 1884 when he appears before the Magistrates Court in Harrow charged with two specimen counts of Burglary Dwelling, although police suspected him of a dozen or more similar offences. Armed with that information the magistrate saw fit to send him to prison for a total of five years, served in the much hasher environment of the adult Pentonville Prison in North London.

He is released early in April 1888 and within only a matter of weeks, and for reasons that even today are not fully understood, he embarked upon a most ungodly murderous spree killing two women in the most grotesque fashion, too graphic to detail here.

He was found guilty of his crimes at the Central Criminal Court and sentenced to death by hanging, sentence to be carried out at HMP Wormwood Scrubs.

At the eleventh hour he was spared when it was successfully argued in the Appeal Court of London that, so horrific were his crimes that only a mad man could have committed them. On the basis that he was clearly of unsound mind he was spared the noose and ordered to be detained at Her Majesty's Pleasure – in the hell-hole that was HMP Dartmoor Prison, desolate and high on the moor at Princetown, Devon.

Save for the brief report from Dr Waterman, the Governor of HMP Dartmoor Prison dated 1st October 1889, there is precious little mention of Selden's escape from custody. We know that at that time inmates were normally kept in squalid condition, four to a cell. Selden had such a violent disposition that he had the luxury of a rat-infested cell all to himself.

We know that he made good his escape between the random headcounts timed at 15.35 hrs when he was spoken to in the prison laundry where he worked, and the next, timed at 19.40 hrs when he was discovered missing from his cell. In his place, officers found a dummy made from prison clothing and stuffed with soiled laundry. Quite how it came to be in his cell, and he missing, has never been determined but it is thought that an accomplice placed the dummy in the cell allowing Selden time to escape under the cover of darkness, probably slung underneath one of the many carriages that enter and leave the prison gates.

It is open to question whether he would have made it safely to South America had it not been for the presence on the moor of Dr Watson and Sherlock Holmes. He had a safe haven at Baskerville Hall and by all accounts would have continued to elude police and prison guards had it not been for the wits of Dr Watson in spotting the signal light from the moor.

And how great a part in his death did wearing Sir Henry's London clothes play. While we know from Dr Watson and Sherlock Holmes' accounts that the Hound was certainly nearby the place where Selden fell to his death, there is still no evidence that Selden was fleeing from it, rather than his human pursuers when he fell.

Indeed, the police acknowledge as much themselves when they concede that there would have been little likelihood of a conviction against Stapleton in relation to any involvement in Selden's death, such was the paucity of the evidence to connect him or his hound to the incident.

Apart from his sister Eliza Barrymore, few it seems mourned his passing and following a post-mortem examination he was unceremoniously buried in an unmarked grave within the walls of HMP Dartmoor Prison. From the original Devon County Constabulary report we can clearly infer that the police view was very much 'good riddance', reference to the fact that they believe he should have felt the noose around his neck after his trial in August.

**The Selden Post Mortem –**

Unlike the case involving Sir Charles, the circumstances surrounding the death of Selden cried out for a post-mortem examination.

Professor Kennedy had two principal injuries to investigate, the fractured skull and the broken neck. Not that it actually mattered, Selden was dead, but it was important to determine the precise cause of death. Again, the Professor would have read the preliminary police notes and completed an examination of the skin noting marks and so on. Next the extent of the visible skull injury would have been explored and measured and precise notes taken before the site of the wound was explored in more detail, the means by which I shall not trouble you with.

Similarly, when investigating the fractured vertebrae the area would have been explored in a sequence or more and more invasive dissection until the spinal cord was visible for inspection.

It is a common misconception that all fractures of the neck prove fatal. Not so, many people can fracture one or more of the vertebrae in their neck and not even know it, others suffer degrees of paralysis if there is trauma to the delicate spinal cord but death occurs where the spinal cord is completely severed.

In such cases the nature of the trauma means that the vital organs are deprived of the signals and impulses from the brain that they require for normal function. This is what happened to Selden in that his neck was broken in the instant that he fell. The fracture to the skull was simultaneous, but the vital clue was in the fact that there was little blood around the fracture site, clear indication that the heart wasn't pumping when the injury occurred. On that basis Professor Kennedy made his determination as to the cause of death, the manner of his death would have been determined as 'accidental'.

**Events in London –**

We have the situation where, almost at the moment Sir Henry resolves to travel to travel to Baskerville Hall, Selden makes good his escape and in so doing brings about the undivided attention of over 100 armed guards from HMP Dartmoor Prison, the majority of whom are dead shots having seen service in the military, together with several hundred police officers, again a good number of whom are trained marksmen. You would imagine that their presence about the moor would have been quite enough to convince Mr Stapleton to delay any notion he might have of removing Sir Henry from the line of inheritance to Baskerville Hall.

That may have been so had Stapleton and his wife not already made the trip to London and were therefore oblivious to events back on the moor. Quite why Stapleton had considered it necessary to travel to London to source something with Sir Henry's scent upon it, when surely it would have been an easier proposition to wait until Sir Henry had ensconced himself at Baskerville Hall at which point Stapleton could have taken any number of items at any moment he chose.

By travelling to London, and of necessity having to take his less than complicit wife along too, he came very close indeed to having his plans discovered, particularly as his wife had taken to warning Sir Henry off, by sending letters to the Northumberland Hotel.

Holmes came very close indeed to stopping Stapleton in his tracks on more that one occasion before leaving Baker Street and even setting foot upon the moor. Indeed, it is more than probable that had Stapleton remained at Merripits House and simply awaited the arrival of Sir Henry, Sherlock Holmes would not have troubled himself to take the case in the first instance.

There was little credibility to be attached to the pleas of Doctor Mortimer in making some emotive connection between some local legend and the untimely (but medically explained) death of a dear friend and local dignitary. There is no doubt that had it not been for the theft of the boot, the charade in the hansom cab and the warning letter, there would have been very little to tantalise and engage the mind of the great consulting detective.

He does though, take the case and as a result his companion Dr Watson is despatched to accompany Sir Henry as he takes up his family seat at Baskerville Hall. Is it some misplaced sense of drama that makes Holmes keep his own travel plans secret, even from his trusted associate, does he simply not think him discreet enough, or can he really even at this very early stage have some inkling as to what is afoot and that the situation demands a degree of secrecy, we will never know.

The Stapletons too have to think on their feet and make a hasty return to Merripits House, after all, not being privy to the conversation over dinner at the Northumberland Hotel their first indication as to what was happening would only have come when Sir Henry, Dr Mortimer and Dr Watson board the train for Buckfastleigh. Once home, we can only imagine what effect the presence of several hundred armed prison guards and police officers searching every inch of the moor would have had on any plans Stapleton might have made. One thing can be sure, their presence would certainly have served to calm any concerns harboured by Dr Watson and Sir Henry.

Of course, not so Selden, evicted from the comfort of Baskerville Hall back onto the moor at the mercy of his pursuers, the same for Holmes, who despite his honest motives could at any time have been mistaken for the escaped felon and shot dead. That he did survive is due in great part to him having the presence of mind to bring young Cartwright down with him from London to act as his runner and an extra pair of eyes.

**The call to Lestrade –**

We move on now to a well documented element of the case, the involvement of Detective Inspector Lestrade at new Scotland Yard.

Despite the fact that the Metropolitan Police was founded as an institution by Sir Richard Mayne in 1839, sixty years on the concept of a separate body being deployed to investigate crimes to the exclusion of all other police duties was still in its infancy and only a few pockets of such specialist officers existed, all based at New Scotland Yard, of which Lestrade was one.

The Victorian era is marked by a broad interest in magic, the supernatural, the unexplained, and it would be natural to assume that for as much as Holmes would naturally be drawn to the world of a real-life detective such as Lestrade, he too would be attracted by the world inhabited by Sherlock Holmes. Inevitably these two would at some stage meet and in time become uneasy bedfellows, Holmes critical of the robotic, methodical methods of Lestrade, he despairing of the rampant, flamboyant style and celebrity of Holmes.

When then, a rather cryptic telegram arrives at New Scotland Yard summoning him to take part in an investigation in Devonshire, it would be hard to resist the opportunity.

Lestrade though, has a problem. At that time it would have been almost unheard of for an officer of the Metropolitan Police Service to work outside of the Metropolitan Police District unless it was at the express request of another force. 'Calling in the Yard' was very much a mixed blessing for smaller forces, for while it provided them the resources to solve the more complex cases it also a highly public acknowledgement that the force concerned 'wasn't up to the job' itself.

In any event, in order to travel the officer concerned, then as today, would have had to submit a request to travel. Officers today have fewer restrictions and are able to cross force boundaries with little or no hindrance, but in the time of Lestrade Chief Constables jealously guarded their fiefdoms and were watchful and very wary of any interlopers, especially from the Metropolitan Police who were considered aloof and elitist, a legacy that persists to this day

It is this very telegram and the bureaucracy that results, that allows us our unique glimpse into the investigation. Without the need for endless reports there would be no official record, we would be none the wiser and the record would have remained incomplete.

The contents are straightforward and tell Lestrade all that he needs to know, a more detailed message would have cost a fortune to transmit and put too much information into the public domain, particularly as the 'interception' of the telegraph was a good source of information for unscrupulous journalists who had paid sources in most of the London telegraph offices.

One curious element is the fact that Holmes clearly states in the telegram that the matter under investigation is a Murder, he then goes on to ask that Lestrade brings with him an arrest warrant. In practical terms a police officer would not need a warrant to affect an arrest for such a serious crime as all police officers were empowered to arrest anyone who they reasonably believed had or was either in the act of committing, or about to commit any arrestable offence, that being any offence punishable with five or more years in prison, something Holmes would be expected to know.

We are left to wonder if this was another example of a gap in Holmes' knowledge of the practicalities of everyday police work; something we already know alienated him in some senior police circles.

Even in such circumstances where a warrant is required, the document has to be presented to a Justice of the Peace together with a sworn 'information', a document which outlines very briefly the available evidence against the accused. Only when it is signed by the Justice does the warrant bestow any powers.

Even today, when a great deal of authority has been delegated to senior police officers J.P.'s around the country can testify to the urgent telephone calls deep into the night and the hushed oaths taken in dimly lit kitchens over mugs of tea at 3am.

**Lestrade requests authority to join Holmes**

On one hand we have Detective Inspector Lestrade, a man who has distinguished himself sufficiently to rise through the ranks, a well educated, intelligent man who plainly has the confidence of his superiors otherwise he would not be trusted for plain clothes duty and the freedom it allows the individual. A freedom that comes with great responsibility, the ability to pass unnoticed among your peers at the same time going about your work, prying and teasing information, flirting with the seedy underbelly of Central London.

On the other hand we have this fellow Sherlock Holmes, a privateer who is dismissed in some police circles as a showman, suspected in others of being in some way complicit in many of the crimes he has 'solved', so complex and seemingly insolvable did they seem to the 'professionals'. When a man like that asks for the assistance of one of your best men, opinion is bound to be divided.

Detective Chief Inspector Kellenson is Lestrade's immediate superior, and on reading his minute to Lestrade's report it is clear that he is not unduly concerned, appears to take matters at face value and approves the request with only one condition, that Lestrade draws a revolver from the armoury.

Kellenson's superior, Detective Chief Superintendent Steel, clearly takes a different view and from his minute, it is clear that he questions the need for Lestrade to 'go it alone' and is insistent that he makes immediate contact with senior officers from the Devon County Constabulary.

The regulations would have required that Lestrade kept note in his official pocket-book of all that occurred from the moment he left London. The rail ticket would have to be kept in order to recover his expenses as would receipts for meals and other refreshments. Sundries such as newspapers would have to be paid for out of his own pocket. Times of departure and arrival would be recorded, persons encountered and places visited, all to be included in any subsequent statement or report.

What none of them were to know was what Holmes had in store, namely a briefing on the investigation to date over a pub meal in Coombe Tracey then straight into action on the moor during which firearms were discharged. Lestrade must have seen his career flash before his eyes at the thought of explaining those events to Detective Chief Superintendent Steele.

**Lestrade on the moor**

With that in mind I sometimes try to put myself in Lestrade's position as he crouched in the rocks at Merripits House, gun at the ready - and it really isn't a nice place to be. His 'friend' Sherlock Holmes has sent an urgent telegram asking him to travel by train to help in a murder investigation. By virtue of the fact that he asked for the help of Scotland Yard means that something out of the ordinary must be involved otherwise the local police would be involved.

On that basis he has just edged the case to be allowed to travel down, armed with a sidearm, and under strict instructions from above to meet end explain all to a senior local CID officer as soon as he can. During the long hours on the train his mind would have been working hard to imagine what the case might be, planning his actions and responses, full of anticipation. The reality though is very different; he is given a few theoretical deductions over a rushed dinner and is straight away pressed into service on some dark, dank moor.

And what of this supposed complex murder enquiry, well the truth appears to be that the three of them are waiting in the cold and the fog, in the shadows, for a savage hound to attack a local landowner. Lestrade could easily have been forgiven for wondering if he had lost leave of his senses in leaving the comfort of his desk in New Scotland Yard. It is quite one thing living and breathing a case for weeks on end, having every minute detail of a case stored away in your head, aware of every detail, the evidence catalogued for instant recall – and quite another to be brought into a case at the very death, totally reliant on those about you. Case in point, when Sir Henry walked past the trio in the fog, Lestrade wouldn't even have known who he was.

In truth, in the end it probably suited Lestrade that Stapleton could not be found. No arrest involved, no paperwork as such, no lengthy witness statements to be made and most importantly, no rail trips back and forth between London and Exeter to give evidence.

The issue of domestic violence between Mr and Mrs Stapleton was also resolved at a stroke by his disappearance and the lingering suspicion that Stapleton had been involved in sporadic, high-value burglaries about the region were solely a matter for the Devon County Constabulary. His only real concern would have been the impending wrath of Detective Chief Superintendent Steel on his return.

## Lestrade returns to London

We know from the report of Detective Superintendent Johns of the Devon County Constabulary that he had a meeting with Lestrade before his return to London. One can only imagine how uncomfortable a situation that must have been for Lestrade. I have no doubt that Johns would have vented some considerable fury at him fort being kept in the dark and any other number of real or perceived sleights. The rare opportunity to round on someone of the rank and stature of Lestrade would have afforded Johns some considerable kudos in local circles.

Little wonder then that in submitting his report on his return to New Scotland Yard, Lestrade refers only briefly to his limited involvement in the case and is keen to have his superiors read instead the report from Detective Superintendent Johns which places events in a more detailed context.

## Devon County Constabulary

I can almost imagine the morning after the Hound was slain and the sudden deluge of work the case created for the normally sleepy world of the Devon County Constabulary.

As far as they were concerned their involvement with the Baskerville family had ended following the inquest into the natural death of Sir Charles Baskerville in May. The fact that Mr Holmes had seen fit to call it murder over dinner in London and then slink about the moor to apprehend the culprit was completely unknown to them, as was the involvement in that investigation, if it could be called such – of a Detective Inspector from the Metropolitan Police in London.

It would have been enough to tax a small constabulary in simply dealing with the escape of such a high-profile convict such as Selden let alone deal with the subsequent fall-out from a case involving such well known figures and a local dignitary.

Without Doctor Mortimer revealing what he thought to police at the time of Sir Charles' death there was little else to be done and the case was closed at the conclusion of the inquest. The quiet routine would have been shattered with the news of Selden's escape, hasty meetings would be called with senior prison staff, and previously agreed search plans put into action.

Officers would have been drafted in from all corners of the county, their duties having to be covered by remaining colleagues – all earning a pretty penny in regulation overtime. Time and a half usually makes for a willing bunch of workers. That would have been until the reality of trudging about the moor in mid-October set in, ill-equipped and rain sodden, Constables living in flimsy tents or abandoned sheds while Sergeants and above were billeted in local digs or better still, in rooms back at Princetown where there were several good inns. Every gully, leat and tinworks shed would be checked and marked off on a grid pattern radiating from the prison in all directions until the entire moor had been searched.

Other officers would be stationed at railway stations and other locations where it might prove easy to board a slow moving train, carriages transporting goods and wares about the area were stopped and searched as were all of the homes and outbuildings. Posters would be handed around in public places and every station in the county would have the latest gazette posted prominently for all to see. In theory, it should have only been a matter of time before Selden was caught. But nobody new that he had been given sanctuary at Baskerville Hall.

Add to the mix the appearance of Sherlock Holmes and the revelation that another murderer, Stapleton, is at large, and it is easy to imagine the state of panic that beset the Devon County Constabulary.

In fact, it was an ideal situation. Selden was confirmed dead and so the target for the searchers was simply substituted and a new grid begun, this time radiating from Merripits House. The necessary resources were there, the men were now accustomed to their task and practiced in their craft and so more likely to find him had Stapleton been at large.

That they found only the missing boot, the Hounds lair and the phosphor preparation prove only to confirm what Holmes had deduced and by no measure prove that Stapleton was lost to the mire.

## Conclusions

Such is the confidence of the Devon County Constabulary in their ability to find Stapleton, (they being unable to find a solitary trace of Selden in two weeks of searching), that they declare the fact that that he had not been found as evidence in itself that he must therefore be dead. I believe this conclusion suited all the parties.

The gathering press were told that Holmes and Dr Watson had been brought in secretly by the Chief Constable to help in the search for Selden, the situation regarding the hound was downplayed and the incident involving Sir Henry was seldom spoken of again.

The closing paragraphs of the report from Detective Superintendent Johns provide a clear idea of just what view was taken of the whole affair. Dr Mortimer would be interviewed regarding his 'inaccurate' statements to the police and HM Coroner; the Barrymores would be interviewed regarding any offences disclosed as a consequence of harbouring Selden, as would Sir Henry for negotiating his safe passage in return for information concerning the letter from Miss Lyons, although I suspect the entire matter, rather like the fate of Stapleton, was left to quietly die away.

Lestrade was given a dressing down before returning to face Detective Chief Superintendent Steele, whom we can see from his closing minute, was very keen to do the same to Sherlock Holmes.

Holmes, as we know, would never succumb to such pressures, he was after all London's singularly most accomplished consulting detective.

# Acknowledgements

I would like to express my sincere thanks to the following bodies and individuals who provided invaluable help in putting this volume together –

**Devon & Cornwall Constabulary Heritage and Learning Resource**
Okehampton Police Station, Exeter Road, Okehampton

**Metropolitan Police Crime Museum**
New Scotland Yard

**Mr Roger Johnson**
Sherlock Holmes Society of London

# Selected Bibliography

**Doyle, A.C.,** 'The Hound of the Baskervilles' in The Penguin Complete Sherlock Holmes-1981 (London, Penguin Books Ltd)

**Weller, P.,** The Hound of the Baskervilles – Hunting the Dartmoor Legend -2001 (Tiverton, Halsgrove)

# Internet Resources

**Wikipedia** – Sherlock Holmes, also, The Hound of the Baskervilles

# Index

*Close to Holmes: A Look at the Connections Between Historical London, Sherlock Holmes and Sir Arthur Conan Doyle*
**by Alistair Duncan**

## ISBN-13: 978-1904312505

*"Alistair Duncan has visited the significant Sherlockian and Doylean London locations and has shared his enthusiasms in this very readable guide…As an informed and unique addition to further our studies, it is a rare treat!"*
**Sherlock Holmes Society of London Journal**
(Summer 2009).


*Aside Arthur Conan Doyle: Twenty Original Tales by Bertram Fletcher Robinson*
**Compiled by Paul R. Spiring**

## ISBN-13: 978-1904312529

*"The collection proves that Fletcher Robinson was more than capable of producing good work and would probably have gone on to greater things had his life not been cut short."*
**The *Weekend Supplement* of the**
**Western Morning News**
(14 March 2009).

*The World of Vanity Fair by Bertram Fletcher Robinson*
Compiled by Paul R. Spiring

## ISBN-13: 978-1904312536

*"Every now and then, you come across a really sumptuous book, where just turning and looking at the pages takes you into another world.  Such is the case with this one."*
**The Bookbag**
(May 2009).


*A Chronology of the Life of Sir Arthur Conan Doyle:*
22nd **May 1859 to 7th July 1930**
**by Brian W. Pugh**

## ISBN-13: 978-1904312550

*"There can be little doubt that this book is one of the most important books on Conan Doyle… As such it is a truly indispensable guide for the researcher."*
**Alistair Duncan**
(May 2009).

***Bobbles & Plum: Four Satirical Playlets by Bertram Fletcher Robinson
and PG Wodehouse***
**Compiled by Paul R. Spiring**

# ISBN-13:  978-1904312581

*"The discovery of four satirical 'playlets' by PG Wodehouse, seen by the public for the first time in 100 years this weekend, prove that the humorist – who is often viewed as apolitical – had a strong interest in public affairs from his youth."*
**The Observer**
(26 July 2009).

***The Norwood Author: Arthur Conan Doyle & The Norwood Years (1891 – 1894)***
**by Alistair Duncan**

# ISBN-13:  978-1904312697

*"Alistair Duncan is one of a distinguished little group whose work takes us just a little closer towards a complete portrait of the man who created Sherlock Holmes."*
**The District Messenger**
(Feb 2010).

*Rugby Football during the Nineteenth Century*
**Compiled by Paul R. Spiring**

## ISBN-13: 978-1904312871

*"There have been some cracking rugby history books down the years, but never have we been treated to rugby writing by the men who were there at the time. Until now."*
**Rugby World Magazine**
**Book of the Month**
(June 2010).

*Arthur Conan Doyle, Sherlock Holmes and Devon:*
*A Complete Tour Guide & Companion*
**By Paul R. Spiring, Brian W. Pugh, Sadru Bhanji**

## ISBN-13: 978-1904312864

*"Some 220 pages are devoted to the Devon tour. Even without the literary interest the tour would be worth undertaking, as the county is so remarkably varied and beautiful, but the chance to walk in the footsteps of Conan Doyle and Sherlock Holmes is almost irresistible. The book's easy readability belies the awe-inspiring amount of research that s gone into it."*
**Sherlock Holmes Society of London**

www.ingramcontent.com/pod-product-compliance
Lightning Source LLC
Chambersburg PA
CBHW080802020726
47502CB00007B/2256